SOUTHERN

GOTHIC

stories

JOHN RYLAND

Southern Gothic

Written by John Ryland

Published by Gnat Smoke Press

10/31/2020

acknowledgments

Some of these stories have appeared in other wonderful journals and publications. I would like to thank them for having faith in me to publish my work and ask that you find these journals and give them a try, they are excellent publications.

The Opening of a Grave appeared in *The Scarlet Leaf Review* in October 2019

I Didn't Come Here to Die appeared in *Potato Soup Journal* in October 2019

The Finger of God appeared in *Otherwise Engaged* in November 2019

Finding Caroline appeared in *The Writer's Magazine* in November 2019

Ollie and the Stickman appeared in *the Eldritch Journal* in February 2020

The editing of these stories was performed by the talented, and eternally patient, Nicole Neuman. Her hard work helped me take the jumbled-up squiggly lines and make them into the stories that I hope you enjoy. I cannot thank you enough, Nicole.

The artwork on the title pages and the cover [was created by the incomparable Novyl Saeed. She is a phenomenal artist who lives in New Zealand. If you'd love to see more of her work, you can find it at lyvOnlyvOn.wixsite.com/lyvOn

I would also like to thank my lovely wife, Terri, and wonderful sons for their patience, love, and support, without which none of this would have been possible.

TABLE OF CONTENTS

Taking Names

"Instead of a closing statement from the defense, the family has petitioned this court for the opportunity to have the accused speak on his own behalf. I have spoken with the defendant and have an idea of what he will say. With that in mind, I have ordered the courtroom closed for the statements, as to not cause further damage to the reputation and memory of the victim."

The judge ran a hand over his thinning hair and looked around the courtroom. The prosecutor sat with the family of Candance Weatherford and the defense attorney sat with the family of Joseph Patrick. The jury looked tired and battered like they'd rather do anything than hear the twelve year old boy speak another word. It was a long and difficult trial, and it was clear that there would be no winners.

The judge looked at Joseph Patrick and sighed. Sitting behind the defense table, the boy looked like any typical kind you'd see at the mall, albeit one who was dressed up for a special occasion. His brown hair was neatly cut, the Windsor knot in his tie was near perfect, and the gray suit he wore fit him well. He'd been quiet and respectful throughout the trial, answering "yes sir" and "no sir" when the D.A. asked questions.

His eyes, however, told a different story. There was no youthful exuberance common in most young boys his age. No zest for life, no look of immortality often found in young, strapping boys. The look in Joseph Patrick's eyes was tired and worried. He looked haggard beyond his years as if a great weight hung on his shoulders. There was sorrow in his eyes, but no remorse.

In his forty years as a judge, presiding over the lives of children who'd run afoul with the law, he'd seen the look before. That was what bothered him. When he'd seen the look before, it was worn by older kids who'd lived a harrowing life or had been subjected to some of the worst depravity imaginable. Something in them had broken and, he guessed, in Joseph Patrick too.

"You may come forward, young man, and address the jury." He sank back into his chair as he watched the boy back his wheelchair back from the table and steer it forward. The kid spared his parents a quick look, giving them a sad smile as he rounded the table.

"I know you've all heard a lot of people talking about me and the things I did. I'm not going to say they didn't happen, but I'm going to tell you *why* they happened. You might think I'm crazy for what I'm about to tell you, but I swear every bit of it is the truth. It may sound unbelievable, and I probably wouldn't believe it either, if I hadn't lived through it." Joseph took a deep breath and swept his eyes over the adults peering down at him from the jury box.

A hushed whisper rolled through the jury, but the judge banged his gavel once and they fell silent.

Patrick cleared his throat and began to speak.

"When Ms. Foley got called to the office, she asked if anyone wanted to watch the class. No one raised their hand, so she picked Candance. She always picked Candance, all the teachers picked her. I guess they trusted her because they could depend on her to rat us out."

The D.A. objected and the judge told Patrick to rephrase his statement.

"I'm sorry, your honor." Patrick swallowed hard and looked at Candance's parents. "I'm sorry." He looked back at the accusing eyes of the jury and sighed.

"Anyway, she was dependable. The teacher told her she could take down the names of anyone who acted out and write them on the board, then she'd deal with them when she got back. Teachers did that a lot, especially when another grown-up wasn't available to watch the class if they were called away.

"I guess kids being kids and all, it didn't take long for people to start getting restless. The first name on the board was Micah Rodgers. He started talking to Amelia Sutter. I think he had a crush on her, you know. She's a cute redhead and a lot of guys have a crush on her. Amy, uh- Amelia, was the second name on the board. After that, the class just settled down for a while, until someone threw a wadded-up piece of paper at me. It was Cooper Newsome and Candance saw him. His name went on the board next. When I got up to pick up the paper, intending to throw it away, my name went up. I thought it was a little petty, but…" Joseph trailed off with a shrug.

"The last name put on the board was a kid named Rodney Andrews. Someone passed gas rather loudly. In the quiet classroom, it was really loud, and a lot of kids laughed. Candance said she saw him lean over to do it, so she put his name on the board. He denied it, but it was probably him. He did that a lot."

Joseph rested his elbow on the arm of his wheelchair and leaned forward, rubbing his forehead. "All that might seem irrelevant to you sitting here today, but it's not. Those five names represent five lives that changed that day, and not for the good."

"Within a week, Amy began to lose her teeth. They just fell out one by one. Her parents took her to the dentist, but he couldn't figure it out. She had nearly perfect teeth, but the roots would die, and they'd just fall out. As you could imagine, her parents were freaking out. They took her to doctors and everywhere they could. Over the next three weeks, every tooth she had fell out, and then the gums started to rot. I called her once, to check on her, and I could barely understand her. They suspected cancer but still haven't found anything. It's like her mouth just started rotting."

Joseph Patrick took a sip of water and looked at the jury.

"Then Micah Rodgers, the kid who was talking to her, woke up with a mouth full of blood. He told me that himself. He just woke up one morning and his mouth was full of blood. It was all over his pillow. When he went to the bathroom and looked, his tongue was bleeding. At first, he thought he'd just bit it in his sleep, but it wouldn't stop bleeding. His parents took him to the emergency room when they couldn't get it to stop. They couldn't find a reason. It was like blood was just seeping out of every pore. They did all kinds of tests and stuff, but they couldn't stop it from bleeding. They sent him to specialists and everything, all the while his tongue just kept bleeding. With no other recourse, they had to cut it off. They had to cut a thirteen year old boy's tongue off. He will never talk again."

Joseph rubbed his eyes with both hands, then pushed them over his hair. "So that's Amy and Micah, whose names were on the board for talking. By this time, her teeth were gone, and her gums were rotting away, and he'd lost his tongue. The next name on the board was Cooper Newsome."

"Your honor," the D.A. said, standing as he waved a hand at Joseph. "I appreciate the court's indulgence of this young man, but the medical situations of other young people have no bearing on this case and aren't pursuant to its timely end. He is on trial for murdering a beautiful young girl in cold

10

blood. Should her parents endure this irrelevant nonsense before justice is wrought by the jury?"

The judge banged his gavel once. "Your objection is overruled. The defense has agreed to use this as a closing statement and has the right to include any exculpatory statements or evidence to that end. You had your chance to object before agreeing to allow the defendant to speak."

"Thank you, sir." Joseph spared his parents a nervous glance, then looked back at the jury. "As I was saying, the next name on the board was Cooper Newsome. He was a pretty good baseball player. He played outfield because he had such a good arm. He was young, strong, and healthy. He was a shoo-in to make the middle school team when tryouts came around.

"But he didn't make the team. He didn't even get a chance to try out. Not long after his name went on the board, he started having pain in his right arm. At first, he just thought he slept on it wrong, or maybe pulled a muscle. It kept getting worse, though. His parents gave him Tylenol or something and didn't pay much attention. Until the knot popped up on his shoulder. They took him to his regular doctor, who sent him to a specialist. An oncologist, I think they're called. It didn't take long to find out that he had cancer. I can't remember the name of it, it's long and hard to pronounce, but it is cancer. That's enough to know.

"Me and Coop were pretty close, so I spent a lot of time talking to him about it. His parents were devastated. He's been depressed and hurting a lot even with the pain pills. They started chemo and radiation. I remember seeing him after one of his trips to the doctor. He lost weight, his hair was falling out, and he had thrown up all over himself."

Joseph shook his head and took a few minutes to compose himself. "Coop was the quintessential athlete. He was tall and strong, had a good build, and was good-looking. He had it all. To be honest, deep down I guess I was always jealous of him. If I tried out for the middle school team, I'd have had a 50/50 shot at making it, but not Coop. He was a pretty cool guy, too. Everyone liked him. He wasn't a jerk like some athletes can be. He was smart and funny too, but the last time I saw him he wasn't any of those things.

"He was pale and skinny, quiet and scared. He was fighting for his life from a cancer that just popped up and was aggressively spreading. To be honest, if he doesn't die, it will be a miracle. His thirteenth birthday was two months ago."

Joseph swept his eyes along the jury box slowly, making eye contact with each member. Some of them returned his stare, convinced of his guilt. Some of them dropped their gaze to their hands, unable to look at him.

"Another name on the board that day was Rodney Andrews. He is a black kid who is ten times smarter than he wants people to know. He always acted like he didn't care about school. Like he wanted some street cred or something. His mother didn't have much money, so he didn't always wear nice clothes with name brands on the label. But he was smart. I learned that last year when we got paired up on a science project. I wanted to do something simple and get it done, but he wouldn't hear of it. We ended up doing a massive project detailing how the introduction of a pack of wolves into

Yellowstone National Park changed the path of the Colorado River. It was amazing, and probably the best piece of schoolwork I've ever done, and it was all because of Rodney Andrews.

"Rodney's name went on the board that day because he farted. As I said, Rodney could have been a straight-A student, but his home life wasn't that great. I've met his mom a few times and she seemed nice enough, but she has to work a lot. Rodney's father wasn't around and the man that lived with them wasn't a super nice guy. He's probably getting settled into his prison cell right about now. Rodney's mom was a nursing assistant at the hospital. One morning when she came home, she found Rodney laying in his bed, naked and barely conscious. It seems that her boyfriend and another man had gotten high, then beat and raped Rodney repeatedly while she was at work. I don't even want to imagine the horror he went through that night.

"He was an innocent kid, just hanging out at home and this happened to him. Completely aside from the humiliation and shame they heaped on him, they also broke his jaw and did significant damage to his, well, you know. He had a couple of surgeries and will probably have more. Right before this trial started, the state people came to take him from his mother and put him in a foster home. I don't even know where he is, and neither does she."

Joseph looked at his legs, sitting limply in the wheelchair for a long time before he began to speak again.

"My name, Joseph Patrick, was also on the board that day. I just got up to retrieve a piece of paper thrown by Micah

13

Rodgers. I was just going to throw it away. I wasn't even talking or acting up. Having my name on the board for simply picking up a piece of paper was bullsh- it was petty if you ask me.

"I guess I'm a pretty good kid," he offered a questioning look at his parents, who forced a smile and nodded emphatically. "I make decent grades, never really get into any major trouble. I do my chores, I do my homework, I hang out with my friends. Pretty average all the way around. I'm not a monster. I ended up in this wheelchair because I picked up a piece of paper."

"Objection, your honor."

The judge banged his gavel once and pointed it at the D.A.

"It's closing statements, sit down. You'll have your chance to refute any claim made here."

Joseph looked back at the jury with a tired sigh. "The last day I walked, I went to talk to Candance Weatherford. See, I put two and two together after Amy and Micah began to have their problems. They both were put on the board for talking and both were having problems with their mouths. When Micah, whose name was on the board for throwing paper, developed cancer in his throwing arm, I knew something was happening and I wanted to stop it. After all, my name was on the board for getting out of my seat.

"I asked Candance if she was doing it somehow. She denied everything and got mad at me. She said I was just jealous because the teachers trusted her and not me. She said if I acted better maybe things wouldn't happen to me, and that everything was just a coincidence. She was pretty upset like I said. Her mother ended up telling me to leave, so I did.

"I was in the middle of the crosswalk at the corner of her block when a car ran the red light and hit me. I remember lying there on the pavement thinking that it was Candance's fault. It didn't seem real. I wasn't in pain. Nothing hurt. It was like I was just lying down. People came running, the driver was hysterical. I remember hearing her screaming. I remember hearing the ambulance coming, the paramedics. I remember riding to the hospital.

"That was when I knew something was wrong. They'd been telling me to lie still, but on the way to the hospital, they kept doing something to my legs and asking if I felt it. I didn't feel it then and I never will. I am twelve years old and I will never feel anything below my waist again. I stayed in the hospital for a while, then went to rehab. None of it worked. I knew early on that I'd never walk again, just like Amy wouldn't be able to talk and Micah would be mute for the rest of their lives. While I was in rehab, Rodney got his punishment for going on the board.

"There's no way Ms. Foley, our teacher, could have known what she was doing when she asked Candance to take names that day. There's no way she could have known that the things that happened would happen because no normal human being would. Through whatever means she has at her disposal, Candance Weatherford caused these acts to happen. Whether through witchcraft, black magic, voodoo, or whatever, there is no doubt in my mind that she did this to us. That's why I had

15

to stop her. She had to be stopped and no one was able to do it but me."

The judge gaveled down a murmur from the jury box and told them to be quiet.

"I know this isn't Salem, Massachusetts and that it's not the 1600s or whatever, but Candance is some sort of witch, nonetheless. You may scoff, and I don't blame you. I wouldn't believe this story if I hadn't lived through it. You may call it coincidence, but every name Candance put on that board has had something horrible happen to them, something that normally doesn't happen to kids. Horrible incidences that just happen to occur to kids whose name Candance wrote that one day."

Joseph unlocked the wheels of his chair and rolled closer to the jury. "There has to be an explanation. If this isn't the right one, then I ask you, what is? What would cause this to happen? What would cause horrible things to happen to five kids, all of which was related to the reason their name was put on the board? What? If not Candance, then who?"

Joseph turned his wheelchair and started toward the defense table, but stopped when the back door to the courtroom opened quietly and a petite, dark-haired woman slipped in. He offered Ms. Foley a sad smile when she looked at him on her way up the center aisle. She offered one of her own and sat down in one of the empty seats.

"Ms. Foley, I have cleared the gallery for closing statements," the judge told her flatly.

"I know, your honor, but I was hoping to be present if I could. I have testified both for and against the defendant, and as the teacher of all six students involved, I feel like I should be present."

"I don't mind," Joseph said with a shrug as he took up his usual position at the defense table.

Mrs. Weatherford stood and addressed the court. "Your honor, if you do not object, I would like Ms. Foley to remain. She has been a stalwart of support for the families involved, especially ours. She has been involved in the trial from the beginning."

The judge sighed and shook his head. "Very well," he said, looking at the teacher, dressed in a black skirt that ended just above her knee and an open jacket that covered a skintight blouse. She was young and attractive, but there was something about her that just didn't feel right with him. "But I will admonish you from speaking to the press or anyone else about the particulars of what is said here today. You are aware of the gag order placed upon these proceedings due to the age of those involved."

"Yes sir, your honor, I am aware."

The judge scratched the bald spot on the back of his head and nodded to the prosecutor to begin. The D.A. stood and approached the jury box, launching into his closing statement.

The judge began to thumb through the file before him. He'd studied it ad nauseam but suddenly felt the urge to review it again, if only to pass the time. The D.A. would have a lengthy closing, covering every scrap of damning evidence against the boy. He was nothing if not thorough.

Turning a page in the file, the judge found himself staring at a photo of the classroom blackboard. The names on it had become familiar to him. Amelia Sutter, Micah Rodgers, Rodney Andrews, Cooper Newsome, and Joseph Patrick. Five names placed on a blackboard by a girl who, if the truth was told, was little more than a snitch.

His brow furrowed as he stared at the names, for the first time noticing something peculiar that he'd overlooked. Five of the names had suffered horribly before Joseph Patrick snuck his father's nine-millimeter pistol and waited for Candance Weatherford to walk out of her house. Five names of young, innocent lives visited by tragedy before Joseph pulled the trigger, killing Candance in her front yard.

The five names: Amelia Sutter, Micah Rodgers, Cooper Newsome, Joseph Patrick, and Rodney Andrews, were all written in the neat, sprawling script of a young woman. He allowed his eyes to trace the near perfect penmanship of the names, following the loopy, smooth scraping of chalk on a blackboard. When he finished the five names, his eyes went to the top of the photograph, to the top of the blackboard.

Watchman: Candance Weatherford

He stared at the writing, obviously written by someone else. The lettering was sharp and hard like the writer was striking the board with the chalk instead of allowing it to flow across it. Who wrote this, he wondered? Ms. Foley?

Looking up, he found her staring at him from her seat. Her lips were pursed slightly, and her left eyebrow arched ever so slightly. When her eyes locked on his, he gasped and felt himself being pushed back in his chair. Summoning what force he could, he ripped his eyes from hers and dropped his gaze to the paper before him.

He took a deep breath to calm himself as the strange feeling began to subside. It felt as if something, or someone, had passed right through him. It felt like *she* had passed through him. Still shaken, he looked around the courtroom in disbelief. No one had noticed. He stole another glance at her but discovered her watching the D.A.

He looked down before she could do whatever she'd done to him again. Looking at the picture, he realized that there were not five names listed on the blackboard of children who had suffered greatly, but six. Candance Weatherford's name was also on the board, put there by Ms. Foley, and she was the only one who had died.

The judge looked at Candance's father, sitting stoically as he watched the D.A. His wife wiped tears as she too watched the man do the job of prosecuting a preteen boy of murder. His eyes then went to Joseph, then his parents. The boy was slumped in his wheelchair, resigned to his fate, while his parents wiped tears from their cheeks as the D.A. recounted the day Candance Weatherford died.

Suddenly, the whole case began to feel dirty, as if justice were being perverted somehow. His eyes went back to Ms. Foley and found her staring at him again. This time he did not look away but returned her knowing stare despite the tingling sensation that was spreading throughout his body. She was pushing him again, but this time he was pushing back. In all his years on the bench, he'd never been stared down, and he had no intention of starting today.

Her stern face softened as a smile spread across her dark lips. She stood, moving in the smooth, unhurried way of a woman confident in her position. She straightened her jacket and gently touched the back of her hair before slipping out of the seat and into the aisle.

The tingling subsided as she moved down the center aisle away from him with a casual, elegant walk that held his attention. When she reached the back of the courtroom, she put a hand against the dark mahogany of the door but did not push it open. Her long fingernails, painted a deep maroon, laid against the wood like claws as she turned to look at him over her shoulder.

When their eyes met again, he felt a sudden push against his forehead as a thought fought its way into his mind: Knowledge can be a dangerous thing. A wise man remains quiet in the face of his ignorance, a fool speaks of things he cannot understand.

Unaware that he was pushing back against the invasion of his mind, his torso lurched forward as the assault stopped suddenly. He took in a deep breath and steadied himself. His eyes, drawn to the woman, fell on her as she waited at the back of the room. She gave him a smile and a quick wink before pushing the door open and slipping quietly from the courtroom.

Painting the Dead

His name was Joe, but nobody knew that. He was just a stranger walking along a darkened road, moving through the lives he intersected like a shadow. Sometimes he was noticed, sometimes not. Of course, that was fine with him. Sometimes it's better not to be noticed.

The canopy of trees closed in quickly, leaving him to find his way along the country road without the view of the sprawling countryside he had been enjoying. He didn't mind the shadows. He'd spent most of his life in the shadows and felt most comfortable there. In the shadows, no one could see his face, especially the long, jagged scar that dominated his left cheek.

He wasn't heading home, or away from home. The truth was that he didn't have anywhere to go or anywhere to be. The last town that had once captured his imagination was miles behind him now, and he was moving to the next. It was that simple. His life was that simple. He was an artist, on the road of life, seeking the perfect subject.

He adjusted the pack slung over one shoulder and stumbled forward. The pack contained everything he had in this world: various tubes of acrylic paint, an array of brushes and blades, his old worn pallet, a change of clothes, and a few odd trinkets he'd collected along his journeys. In his pocket, he carried thirteen dollars and twenty-nine cents, remnants of the sale of his last painting. That had been months and many miles ago. He needed to create a new masterpiece, and that would take inspiration.

Just now, he thought, his art was being displayed on the wall of some nice upper-class home. Maybe with an art lamp directed on it or featured over the mantle in someone's den. It was warm and safe, out of the elements- unlike the artist. But it was the art that lived forever, not the artist. That was how it should be. The art was the message, he was just the messenger.

Joe stepped onto the shoulder, softened by the morning's rain to allow the vehicle approaching from behind, to pass. Whoever was driving was going the same direction as he, but in a much bigger hurry. He didn't bother to turn back to look and had no intention of doing so. He wasn't hitch-hiking, he was simply traveling. He wouldn't stick out his thumb and hope for the kindness of a stranger to get him where he was going. The journey was part of the adventure that had become his life. The journey would give him time to think and empty his head so that when the next inspiration struck, he'd be ready.

He threw up a wave as the SUV raced past, not even slowing a little. He couldn't tell if the driver waved back, but it didn't matter. He wished them well even if they didn't reciprocate. The vehicle continued down the road and was soon just a pair of taillights, then they too disappeared into the night like so many before them.

He was alone again with the country road and his thoughts.

Cresting a small rise, the trees opened up to sprawling fields on both sides of the road. He allowed his eyes to wash over the vast grassland, picking out dark shadows that moved slowly and ate grass. The faint smell of cattle danced gently on the air, reminding him of his uncle's farm. A smile of fondness came to him as the days of his youth, long spent, came back to him.

The road fell gently away beneath his feet, leading him across the open plain. Walking would be easy for a while and the absence of trees lent more light to the countryside. Along with the cows, he could smell freshly cut hay, and a newly plowed field. The earthy smells entered his body through his nose and spread like a shot of good whiskey until he was consumed by them. They warmed his soul with their genuineness, their truth, and their simplicity. They were life and he devoured their presence. So many things in life were lies. Peace, love, happiness, all lies. These smells: being right here, right now, that was the truth.

To his left, his eyes fell on a narrow track that meandered its way across the land and ended next to a small farmhouse. In the twilight, he could only tell that it was a light color, but his heart begged for it to be yellow. A yellow house with white trim, and maybe green shutters. That would be perfect. Iconic. Steeped in rich symbolism.

A pick-up truck and a car sat beside the house, left out in the night like him.

Joe paused, drawn by the simple beauty of the farmhouse sitting in a field against the darkened hills in the distance, silhouetted against a sky still light enough to show him the lines of the house. While he watched, a light came on, forming a rectangular beacon of yellow in his darkening world. He waited, like a moth, to see what the light would reveal.

Inside the house, a woman young and well-shaped was putting out a setting for two on a wooden table. Her thick, dark hair was pulled back, revealing a slender neckline. The smile she wore signaled youth and innocence; happiness that he missed.

A longing tugged at his heart. A mundane ritual that the woman, and almost assuredly the man as well, took for granted embodied the sense of home to him. A simple, home-cooked meal and someone to eat it with, in a happy home bathed in golden light against a moonless night.

Oh for a canvas, he thought, to preserve this moment, this feeling. Yes, he could recreate the scene from memory. The house, the window, the light, and darkness, but he couldn't recreate the feeling in his chest. He couldn't recreate the longing. The pang of envy.

He stood in the shadows and watched the couple enjoy their meal, imagining their conversation. A silent intruder, he inspected the graceful way she moved and the gentleness of her laugh and pondered the sound of her voice and the smell of her perfume. Did the husband appreciate the gifts he'd been given? Did he cherish her? Did he strive to satisfy her the way she satisfied him? Was either of them aware of the idyllic setting their lives had become? Right here, right now, they were the very picture of the American dream.

They were a Norman fucking Rockwell painting and didn't even know it.

Joe's eyes went to the driveway and his heart began to race. Would an uninvited guest ruin the moment, or would they welcome a stranger into their home? Would a passerby be greeted with hospitality or be turned away? Would this perfect slice of Americana accept him?

No, he thought, his eyes narrowing. They would surely turn him away.

His eyes followed the woman as the couple finished their meal, watching as the husband rose and planted a kiss on her cheek before disappearing. Joe studied the young wife as she cleared the table and took the dishes into the kitchen.

She would wash dishes in the sink and dry them, putting them away while he watched television. Later on, they would go to bed and the husband would probably want sex. Grunting and groaning on his beautiful bride until he'd finished his business, then he'd fall asleep.

He wouldn't admire her lean body the way it should be admired. He wouldn't kiss her supple neck, losing himself in the rapture of the faint smell of her perfume. He wouldn't revel in the ability to please her, to bring her to the ecstasy she deserved. He would do none of these things because he was selfish and didn't deserve such a lovely creature. He was a brute that made a living strong-arming cattle and throwing hay bales. He knew of no refinements like the scent of a beautiful woman or the gentle curves of her body.

The dumb farmer didn't deserve her, not like he did. He deserved the scene before him. He deserved her.

Joe drew in a deep breath to contain his excitement. He wiped his sweaty palms on his shirt and listened for a moment to his heartbeat thundering in his ears. This moment was almost as good as what would come later. This moment of decision, of anticipation. The build-up to the exquisite release. The warmth of his excitement spread through him like a good whiskey, spreading from his chest until it enveloped his whole being. He closed his eyes, enjoying the moment. When he opened them again, he'd made his decision.

He unslung the pack from his back and opened it. Running his hand inside carefully, his fingers danced around the objects, finding the handle of the butcher's knife. Pulling it from the bag, he stared at the sharp edge of the blade. Twisting it back and forth to catch the faint light, a crooked smile slid across his lips.

He closed his eyes and took in a deep breath to prepare himself. He spared another look at the quaint farmhouse and marveled at how unsuspecting the inhabitants were. Just another Thursday evening. The day was almost done. A few hours relaxing in front of the tube, maybe a quick bout of sex, then a good night's sleep.

They were completely unaware of what lurked just beyond their peaceful little home, beyond the reach of the yellow porch light. Just like so many before them.

He slid a thumb along the blade, checking it for sharpness though he knew it was honed to a razor's edge. The steel sliced into his skin, awakening his mind to the possibilities.

Joe's eyes followed the woman as she crossed the house from left to right, switching off the light in the kitchen. She crossed the dining room and entered the living room. Her shape was barely visible in the faint light of the television through the sheer curtains, but there was no doubt of her presence. She was there, he could feel her presence. She was there, but not. Just like so many other women that had temporarily occupied part of his life.

He stood in the darkness, paused at the intersection of life and death. The words of an old Doors song came to him and he began to slowly mumble the tune while he ran his thumb back and forth across the blade. "The future's uncertain… and the end is always near."

He could walk away, leaving the couple to their picturesque life. They would never know what danger lurked outside in the dark or how close they came to living their worst nightmare. In a few years, they might have kids, watch them grow up, and leave. They might grow old together, in love, and become a couple that everyone envied. Or they might drift apart, their own lives consuming them until they were more roommates than a couple, forgetting their love and the days spent in this tiny farmhouse.

Time had a way of altering the trajectory of things. Time was the real villain.

Which ending would be more savage, crueler? What picture would capture the truth better? Was it better to capture the essence of who they were now, like a butterfly in a jar, and preserve it forever or leave them to an uncertain future?

He could immortalize them in a timeless display of art, or he could leave them to slowly fade into oblivion. She could stay forever young and beautiful in his art, and he strong and masculine, or they could tread upon the years until they were old and feeble, shadows of the people they are right now.

He drew in a deep breath and exhaled slowly.

As he started down the driveway, his palm began to sweat in anticipation around the knife handle. His heart pounded in his ears as everything else began to disappear except the tiny farmhouse and the young couple who resided therein.

"It's okay. Everything's going to be okay," he whispered into the darkness. "I'll make you beautiful again. You'll be beautiful forever now. Forever.

In the back of his mind, the same old Doors song began to play again, and he smiled.

Silas and the Siren

Silas Smith pushed his robust form up from his desk chair with a reluctant groan and rounded the old, faded countertop in the lobby of his aging motel. He went to the front door to flip the equally old and faded sign from "OPEN" to "CLOSED."

Sparing a glance out the window, he watched the rain pound the nearly empty lot, collecting in the potholes out near the road. Two beat-up work trucks were parked on the far side of the lot, on the other leg of the U made up of three one-story buildings. Beneath one of the security lights, he could see the mud being washed from them onto the pavement below. It would be one hell of a mess by morning. The crew being here all week would help him keep the bills paid another month, but he doubted they'd work tomorrow. The rainy spring season had to make it tough to make a living in their business.

His eyes went to the tall, neon palm tree in the forefront of the lot, near the deserted two-lane blacktop that led to the interstate. It always made him happy to see the green neon light up in the shape of palm fronds sitting atop the yellow tree. The trunk was bent inward, toward the building, its fronds hanging over the words "Palm Tree Motel" glowing in white neon. To him the sign was iconic. It advertised air-conditioned rooms and color television, linking it to the days before such amenities were staples in American homes.

The Palm Tree had seen better days and Silas knew that he couldn't compete with the new high-rise hotels. Hell, he didn't even have free Wi-Fi. He and his motel were on a gradual slide and he knew it. It was sad, but it was the truth. Now, most of his traffic was either out-of-town workers looking for cheap rooms or people who needed privacy for a few hours. He refused to rent a room for half-day or hourly rates, as some of the other older hotels did. The way he saw it, if people wanted to screw around on their spouse, or enjoy the company of a professional, they'd have to pay a full day. Sometimes they complained but they paid anyway.

Just as he was about to turn away, a car rolled into the lot. It went directly to the spot in front of room 114. He recognized the late model Sedan as belonging to the customer he'd rented the room to earlier. He was a tall man, but scrawny, with a desperate look in his eyes and a patchy beard on his chin.

He walked in and said he needed a room. Silas pointed to the handwritten sign on the counter explaining that he was mute but could help any customer with anything they needed. The man read the note, grunted, and looked back at him with a perturbed expression. He held up one finger, then stabbed it toward the row of keys on the pegboard behind the counter.

Silas turned, put his hand on the last key, and gave his customer a questioning shrug of his shoulders. The customer went back to the door, looked at the row of doors across the parking lot, and motioned for Silas to move down the row of keys. Finally, he stopped him as his hand reached 114. He returned to the counter and pointed again to the key, signaling that he wanted one room. He then held up one finger again and closed his eyes, tilting his head slightly to one side. He wanted the room for one night, and apparently, he wanted some privacy.

Silas nodded and returned to the counter with the key, pointing to another sign taped to its chipped surface. ONE ROOM, ONE NIGHT $49.99. CHECKOUT AT 11:00.

The man read the sign and gave him the same perturbed look as before like he was considering punching him in the face. He pulled out his wallet, produced three twenties, and dropped them on the counter before snatching the key from Silas' hand. He turned and walked away without registering. Silas considered pressing the issue but decided against it. He'd paid in cash. That was always good. The guy was probably going to have some fun with a hooker, and they'd be gone in a few hours.

Watching from across the lot, Silas confirmed that the man had company, female company, and smiled. The girl, much thinner than what he would prefer, got out of the car and walked casually to the sidewalk. She joined the man by the door, pausing to hold her hand beneath the torrent of rain pouring over the edge of the roof.

While Silas watched, she spoke to the man, but he was busy getting the key into the door lock. He pushed a hand through his greasy black hair and kicked the bottom of the door to room 114. Holding it with one hand, he motioned her inside with the other.

Silas hastily locked his door and switched off the lights. Skirting the counter, he passed the key rack and headed for the door to his room. His heart was already beginning to race with anticipation. It had been more than a week since he'd had any female customers or even male customers with female "friends," but he had one tonight. The girl had blond hair that looked like it came straight from a bottle, but she would do just fine.

A few minutes later, the chair in his bedroom groaned as Silas lowered his considerable girth into it. He sat his can of beer and bologna sandwich down next to his keyboard, pushing a box of tissues out of the way with his plate. He pulled himself to the desk with a hungry smile. With a few strokes of the keys, the computer screen went from black to show the interior of room 114, looking down from the ceiling at the two queen beds.

The room was empty. The single lamp between the beds was on. Neither of them had been turned down, which was typical. On the left edge of the screen, the bathroom door was partially opened. The light was on and he could see shadows moving around. Someone was taking a shower, he thought with a smile. Maybe two someones.

He settled into the chair and picked up his sandwich, content to wait for the show. It would happen, it always happened. And when it did, he'd have a front-row seat.

Chewing on the last bite of his sandwich impatiently, his eyes glued to the screen before him in the otherwise dark room, Silas drummed his fingers against the beer can he held resting on the arm of his chair.

What the hell was taking so long? Sure, make the tramp take a shower, but how long did that take? As he stared at the empty room a disappointing possibility arose in his mind. What if this guy just wanted a quickie in the shower and a good night's sleep? That would suck.

As he took a long drink of his beer, Silas was rewarded with movement in the room. The bathroom door opened wider, and a blonde female sprang into view, completely naked. She paused and looked back at her partner seductively.

Silas smiled. The video was black and white, and grainy, but it was good enough. The petite female had small, but nicely rounded breasts and long, toned legs. Not exactly his cup of tea, but she was still nice to look at. He preferred a woman with more substance, more meat on her bones.

The smile widened on Silas' thin lips as he watched the customer move to the foot of the bed and slowly begin to undress. He had a good angle whichever bed they used, but the one nearest the bathroom was the one most people used.

Switching his beer to his left hand, Silas shifted in his chair to get more comfortable as his excitement grew. Watching wasn't always fun. Sometimes the people were boring or went straight to bed. But tonight's show promised to be different. There was a different feeling about these two, more specifically the woman. She moved with the graceful fluidity of a princess and he was a crass jerk. They made quite an interesting pair.

Silas looked at the man closely, noticing that the scrubby growth of beard was gone. Had he shaved it for her? That was odd. Hookers usually only requested their money upfront and never seemed particularly concerned with facial hair.

The woman's face, calm and passive, looked like she'd been around the block a time or two, but there was a certain beauty to it, a sense of calm that he found comforting. Silas watched with a lustful grin, wishing he were the customer as he pulled the woman to the edge of the bed and began making love to her.

Silas sat in the silence of his dark room and watched the live stream from room 114, his breath coming in rapid pants as he grew more excited.

He looked directly at the back of the customer and noticed for the first time how muscular and toned, almost statuesque, his form was. His firm, round buttocks flexed and relaxed in a steady, effective rhythm. His sense of arousal was both surprising, and yet somehow satisfying as he watched the man's muscles clench and release with each thrust. He was a perfect form of the human body. He was almost as pleasing to watch as the girl was. Almost.

Leaning forward to get a closer look at his screen, Silas felt his heart beginning to race again. The taboo of watching the man was beginning to excite him. With one trembling hand he reached out and touched the screen.

As his fingers met the man's form on the screen, the man in the room stopped suddenly and turned his head, looking directly at the camera, at him. Startled, Silas fell back into his chair, his eyes locked in a silent stare with his customer.

The weight of the man's stare was heavy, almost overpowering him as he tried to shrink further from the screen. Finally, after a few unnerving seconds, the man on the screen smiled at him before turning back to the girl.

He stepped back from her and pushed her around the bed and joined her along the side, giving Silas a perfect view. A smile returned to his face as he sat up in his chair. There was no way the guy could have known about the cameras. He'd been meticulous in hiding them in the smoke detectors.

Silas shrugged dismissively. Whatever the reason, he now had the view he wanted.

The woman's face, limp and expressionless lay facing him. She looked to be peacefully sleeping, if not for the movement of being banged against so hard. Her features were gentle and soft, more like a model than a hooker's. Her smooth features lent her more of a girl next door look than a streetwise prostitute.

Drawing closer to the screen again, Silas allowed himself a moment of wishful thinking. How great would it be to have a woman like this on his arm, to be his girlfriend, his lover? He imagined her being attentive to his needs, eager to please him in a demure, feminine way that he'd never had before. She didn't look the type to be in a cheap motel being mashed by this beast of a guy.

Suddenly the woman's eyelids flew open and she stared back at him. A quick flash of light made her pupils glow green and then was gone. Her face contorted into an angry scowl as her lips parted, revealing two rows of sharp, jagged teeth that more closely resembled rusty nails than anything else.

Recoiling, Silas looked at the customer. Enthralled in his vigorous activity, he hadn't noticed that she'd awakened. His eyes swept back to the woman's face, still twisted into a scowl. She turned her head slowly, looking up at the man above her as he continued his labor.

Her movements were slow and deliberate as she drew the man to her. Her hair began to float as if under water, while the overused bedspread beneath her began to shimmer in the dim light. As he stared at his computer screen, his nose inches from it, the room became filled with a moving, undulating light transforming it into a shallow sea on a sunny day.

The woman allowed her face to fall back to the bed, her eyes finding him again. The scowl was gone, replaced with a sadness that fell upon him like a weighted blanket. The pain in her eyes called to him silently. Was he going to come to her or not? Was he going to be her hero?

Pushing his chair back, Silas stood, unsure of what to do. The urge to rush to her defense was strong, but the man in the room would certainly beat him to a pulp. He was big and strong and probably on something that would allow him to go so hard for so long. He knew he wouldn't stand a chance against a guy like that. And there was the whole scene in the room. What had they done to the lights to get that effect? The fleeting thought that something paranormal was going on entered his mind but was quickly overwhelmed by his desire to possess the girl.

What could he do? Call the police? How would that even work? He did have the type-to-talk software on his computer in the lobby, which also ran his phone. But what would he tell them? That he was secretly spying on some guests and saw them engaging in rough sex. Spying on customers wasn't exactly standard protocol in the hotel business. He'd be labeled a pervert and the Palm Tree would plunge into bankruptcy, not that it had far to fall.

Sitting back down, he clasped his fingers over his protruding stomach and stared at the screen, unsure what to do. As he watched the woman, a sense of duty and responsibility began to rise in his chest again, building a feeling of strength and vigor within him. The voice of newfound confidence told him he could have this woman if he wanted her. She was already his, all he had to do was take her.

Standing suddenly, he went into the bathroom and looked at himself. His face looked thinner, more masculine. He rubbed each of his cheeks as he moved his head from side to side. A smile slowly slid across his face as a sense of euphoria washed over him. He felt more alive than he had in years, but why? Was it the sense of nobility for deciding to help the girl? Could an act of heroism affect him so much?

He ran a hand through his hair and found it healthy and soft. The thick, greasy slab that he usually just brushed to the side was gone. Taking another look in the mirror, he smiled at the strong features now on his face as his skin began to take on a healthy, tanned glow. He was a man of action and his time was now.

He walked back into his bedroom and looked at the scene on the screen. The man was still performing admirably, but when he looked at the woman, she smiled at him and extended a hand beckoningly towards him. It hovered above the shimmering pool of crystal-clear water that had been a bed moments ago, calling to him with a smooth liquidity, inviting him to come to her now. She needed him. She wanted him. Now.

Silas grabbed his beer can and finished the last half of it. He spun on his heels and left the bedroom; his purpose was clearer now than ever.

On the screen in front of the now-empty chair, the scene in room 114 began to change. The woman's fingernails grew into sharp talons, their curves matched the smile on her face. Oblivious to the changes, the man, now a perfect specimen of the human male, his body drenched in sweat, his face a mixture of unbridled ecstasy and agonizing pain, arched his back violently and emptied himself into the woman. The video caught his silent scream as he released the swarm of flies from his trembling body. They poured from his gaping mouth and formed an expanding pool on the ceiling before slowly fading into dark ash and falling from the air, disappearing as they hit the floor.

Reaching up with both hands, she slid her new claws down his body, leaving four long, fine scratches along each rib cage. Exhausted and purged, the man's chin dropped to his chest. His hands dropped to his side as his form slumped before her. Reaching up with her right hand the woman placed one long claw beneath his chin and lifted his head.

"Do you want to come with me?" she asked, in a voice that sounded like the tide rolling on a beach. The man nodded, unable to speak. She smiled knowingly and began to sink into the water, bringing the man with her. Water rushed over the two naked bodies as they slipped beneath the gently lapping waves, sinking deeper and deeper until the darkness enveloped them.

Silas' heart pounded against his chest and reminded him of the bass drums played in the marching band in high school. Of course, he played the tuba, but the drumbeat's reverberations always felt good to him. He could feel the massive amounts of testosterone and hormones being pushed through his body by that beating heart. The vague worry of a heart attack drifted into his mind, but it didn't stay long. He felt too virile, too alive to be dying.

As he walked down the covered sidewalk connecting the rooms, he ran his hands over his chest and found it protruding, firm and strong, beneath his shirt. He also discovered that his usually distended belly had shrunk and was growing flatter by the minute.

An excited chuckle escaped his now chiseled jaw as a bolt of lightning flashed across the sky, accompanied by a crack of thunder. My God, he thought, how good must I look? He paused to adjust himself in his pants, his excitement barely containable beneath the thin khakis. This was already the best night of his life, despite the thunderstorm.

Stopping in front of room 114, he raised a hand to knock on the door but hesitated. The muscles in his forearm rippled beneath smooth, beautiful skin and led to a bulging bicep. Shaking his head with an arrogant smile he lowered his hand and threw a shoulder against the door. It was his door and his motel. He could knock it in if he wanted to and there wasn't shit anyone could do about it.

Stepping into the room, he surveyed the scene. The woman, now fully awake, lay on the bed, the magnificent form of her naked body in full display just for him. She looked different somehow but was even more beautiful in person.

Tearing his eyes away from her, Silas found the customer slumped in the corner, thin and flaccid; completely spent. The skin covering his hollow shell was yellow and rough, like ancient parchment. His opened eyes stared back at him cold and empty from a thousand miles away. The customer, a much less imposing man that he thought, was also soaking wet.

The feeling of a gentle hand caressed his face before slowly drawing his attention to the woman on the bed. She wasn't close enough to touch him, but he could feel her. She lay before him, welcomingly and Silas knew he'd never be able to resist her. That didn't matter because he didn't want to resist her. He wanted to be with her, to possess her, more than he'd ever wanted anything and he was helpless to deny it. He could already feel her presence within him, racing through his veins as if searching for something important. Her heart was beating with his, her lungs were within him, breathing with him.

Pulling his shirt off, Silas revealed his new, chiseled physique. She smiled approvingly as her tongue traveled across her red, pouty lips hungrily. She raised a petite, gentle hand, offering it to him. He immediately approached the bed, eager to serve.

She sat up and unbuckled his belt, again moving as if floating in an invisible pool. His pants sank to the floor without a sound.

The woman lay back on the bed, peering up at him with piercing blue eyes. She shifted her hips, now full and rounded, to align with his. She couldn't have been more perfect if he'd built her himself.

Answering her silent call, Silas stepped forward. She arose effortlessly from the bed to meet him, water cascading down her naked body. His mind exploded with ecstasy as their lips met, sending him to a place he knew he'd never be able to leave.

"Nirvana," was the last coherent thought that went through his mind, and the first intelligible word that had crossed his lips since he was six years old. With that, he slipped beneath the waves of immeasurable pleasure.

Everything he'd ever wanted to be was here. Everything he'd ever wanted to do was here. Every disappointment vanished; every failure faded. His body rejoiced in the newfound pleasure she'd given him. He was perfect. She was perfect. They were perfect together.

The siren waited patiently as Silas exorcised his demons, reassuring him when his insecurities floated to the surface of his semi-conscious mind. After he satisfied himself physically, he began to cry and she comforted him lovingly, hiding her disgust for him behind an irresistible smile. It was a trick perfected over many years. She could be whatever they needed her to be, fulfill their every desire, satisfy their every lust. Then they would willingly surrender their very soul to her, and she would consume it with delight.

The elders had always used the sea to purify their victims, drawing them in and drowning them while they fell in love. It was easy and effective, but inefficient. They only managed to purge the physical bodies of the men back then. Now, she cleansed their souls, exorcised all their insecurities, fulfilled their fantasies, rid them of the foul-tasting shame and degradation they carried around until she was left with a pure, clean, joyous soul. One man cleansed in such a way could take the place of a whole ship of filthy men slowly drowned in the sea.

The computer screen in Silas Smith's bedroom captured its owner as he lay beside the woman, her long claws moving gently along his body, leaving tiny ribbons of blood wherever she touched. It recorded every act under the moon's waning light while the woman waited patiently, like a spider, as the hours crept past.

Lying on a pool of shimmering water, the woman opened her mouth and spoke to Silas as she placed one long claw beneath his chin. He nodded eagerly as her hair began to float on the water. A smile slipped across her lips as she slowly began to sink beneath the rippling waves, her eyes open to watch him follow. The camera captured one last glance from the siren just before the water rushed in to cover them, then went black forever.

Sliding the skin-tight mini dress down over her body, the woman bent closer to the mirror and brushed a stray lock of blonde hair out of her face. Her bright red lips smiled approvingly at her reflection, then faded quickly as her eyes went to the reflection of the two wet bodies slumped in the corner of the room. They were a hideous reminder of what she was, and she'd never quite gotten used to seeing them afterward. The one thing the sea had always afforded her was the easy disposal of her work.

Crinkling her nose, she headed for the door that was now hanging slightly ajar on its hinges. She allowed herself one more last glance at her victims, then switched off the light and left the room. There was no need to clean up. She'd be a thousand miles away before they found the bodies.

Standing on the covered sidewalk outside room 114 at the Palm Tree Motel, she surveyed the lot. A smile parted her ruby lips when her eyes fell on the two work trucks parked across the lot. She cleaned a smudge of lipstick from the corner of her lips with one perfectly manicured nail as her eyes focused on the cheap stucco walls outside the room, announcing her arrival.

She smoothed the dress over her ample hips and started across the parking lot, relishing the water as it fell from the sky. Her stiletto heels echoed in the pre-dawn light despite the standing puddles that covered the parking lot.

Across the lot, before her, a light suddenly came on in the room next to the work trucks.

Ollie and the Stickman

Olivia Hayden watched the school nurse smear anti-itch cream over the small stickman figure she'd drawn on the inside of her left wrist, and the rash that now surrounded it. The nurse taped a bandage over it to keep her from scratching it further and looked up at her.

"I hope you learn a lesson from this, Ollie. Ink is meant for paper, not skin."

"Yes ma'am," Olivia replied flatly, convinced that the ink hadn't caused the rash. It hadn't bothered her for the three classes after English., It only began to itch after she'd bumped into Julie Armistead in the hallway. Dressed in her usual head-to-toe black, long dark hair hanging in strings from her head, Julie of the black lipstick and pale white skin variety.

"Watch out, weirdo," she said to Julie after almost dropping her phone.

True to her usual anti-social form, Julie had taken her arm, looked at the stick man, and mumbled a few words of gibberish, then winked at her and smiled before walking away as if nothing had happened. Shaking her head as she watched her go, Olivia's right hand went to her wrist and started scratching the stickman, now suddenly itching like crazy. She walked to math class fighting the urge to scratch and despising Julie even more.

"What happened to your arm, sweetie?"

Olivia shrugged at her mother. "I don't know. It just started itching so I went to the nurse."

A fire of alarm lit in Brenda Hayden's eyes as she went to her daughter, now shrugging off her backpack onto the kitchen table. "Let me see? Is it a reaction?"

"I don't know, mom," Olivia whined, allowing her mother to take her arm. "It's okay, really."

Brenda looked at her thirteen-year-old daughter's arm, then her face, then her arm again. "What is this?"

"It's a rash, mom. That's why I went to the nurse."

"I see that it's a rash, but what's this?"

Olivia looked down at the edge of the bandage. Her eyes locked onto the stickman doodle. "It's a stickman I drew, but it's moved!"

"Don't be a smarty, Ollie."

"I'm not, mom. Seriously. The stickman was in the center of the rash. I thought it caused it, so did the nurse."

Brenda sighed and shook her head. "Just wash it off, okay. It's been a long week and I want to enjoy the weekend. The rash looks like it's going away. You'll be fine."

Olivia walked to the window, allowing the sunlight to fall on the stickman. Had the stickman moved or did the rash just go away around it? She shook her head as she studied it carefully.

At least the itching had stopped.

"Oh yeah," her mom called from the other room, "We're going out to eat tonight at that new Italian place. It's kinda nice so you'll want to change."

"Okay, mom," Olivia called, still staring at the stick man. "I'm watching you, little man," she whispered to the stickman.

Olivia hid her arm in her lap, her forearm up, so she could keep an eye on the stickman. He'd already moved another inch up her arm since she'd gotten home from school. None of it made sense. Something was wrong, but what? She didn't know what was happening, but it wasn't normal.

She stole a glance at her mother, working on her second glass of wine. Telling her would be useless. She'd already dismissed her earlier. Now they were in a nice restaurant. It was best not to make a scene.

When the waiter appeared with their food, he placed a steaming plate of lasagna before her, warning that the plate was hot. She looked at her delicious food, then to her arm that rested just beside it. What would happen, she wondered. What would happen if she touched the stickman with the hot plate? Would he jump? Would he move away?

She slid her arm closer to the plate, but the stickman didn't move. She moved it closer still, bringing it very close, but not touching the plate. The stickman stood motionless, but his arms were now crooked so that the end of the thin lines rested on his hips.

Olivia swallowed hard and forced herself to look away. "It looks really good," she said, hoping her voice didn't belie her racing heart. "This is a nice place, dad."

"It is. I like it." He smiled and motioned for the waiter to bring him another beer. "Food looks delicious."

"Since it's such a nice place, maybe we should use our manners," her mother said, wagging her finger at Olivia's arm resting on the table.

"Oh, sorry." Olivia slid her arm gently along the hot plate as she removed it from the table, gritting her teeth as the plate touched her skin. Stealing a glance at her arm as she cut her food, she saw a thin, red welt already beginning to form on her skin, but the stickman had moved. He didn't move toward her elbow, but the top of her arm, away from the heat of the burn.

So, she could affect its movements.

Olivia plopped down on her bed and took out her phone. She snapped a few pictures and reviewed them, expanding the image. It was just a stick man drawn in black ink. Although it had moved further up her arm, it was still the same half-inch tall as she'd drawn him. At least it wasn't getting any bigger.

She sighed and stared at the image, wondering what the hell was going on. The whole notion was crazy, but here it was. As much as she wanted to deny it was happening, she couldn't.

"Is there any way to stop you?" she asked in a whisper.

An idea came to her and she smiled. Digging a pen out of her backpack, she drew a circle around the figure and nodded.

"Let's see you get out of that," she said with a triumphant smile, but her victory was short-lived. Her eyes widened as the figure began to walk to the edge of the circle. It made its way around the perimeter, pushing at the ink line she'd drawn.

"Gotcha," she said aloud. "Now you just settle down."

The stickman moved to the part of the circle closest to her and began to push against it. The circle bowed out slightly but held. He pushed harder. The circle bulged more but still held.

Olivia's smile faded as she watched the figure struggle against the edges of the circle. "You're a determined little bugger aren't- ouch!" Her hand went to her forearm, rubbing the searing pain that suddenly began along the edge of the circle in front of the stickman. When she removed her fingers, a section of the circle was gone and so was the stickman. A small bruise was already forming around the broken line.

Gasping, she turned her arm over, searching for him. She found it on top of her arm, standing with his arms crossed as he looked up at her.

"Why'd you do that for?" she asked. The figure didn't answer.

"Why are you here?" she asked. "What are you going to do?" Fear crept into her voice, and her mind as the realization that the words that Julie Armistead mumbled might have been a curse. A real curse!

Olivia grabbed her phone and found Julie's number. "What did you do to me?" she texted.

A smiley face emoji was the only response.

"I've got a rash now. If you don't tell me, I'll tell my mom and she'll call your mom."

An emoji of a hand flipping her the bird showed up on her screen.

Olivia groaned angrily and dropped her phone. The stickman hadn't moved since his escape. That was good, but she wanted him gone. But how? She'd have to get the ink off somehow. Chewing absently on a thumbnail, her mind raced to find a solution.

"There," she said as she placed the last Band-Aid on her arm, completing the ring that went all the way around her forearm, in front of the stickman. "Now what are you gonna do?"

She settled back on the bed and grabbed her phone, intent on filming the figure if he moved again. She centered the stickman on her screen and waited. If he moved at all, she'd have proof.

After a few minutes of filming the motionless stickman, she sighed and shook her head. "You're a clever little guy, aren't you?" she asked. Relaxing into the pillows, she resigned herself to a long wait. Her phone still had half a charge, so she had plenty of time.

"I will catch you," she said, stifling a yawn. "I got all night."

Olivia woke to a sharp pain in her arm. She sat up in bed and immediately looked for the figure. He was standing just past the barricade she'd built, his arms raised in victory. Just behind him, an adhesive end of one of the band-aids stood puckered and stuck to itself. He'd pried it off her skin somehow.

She stared at him as desperation and fear began to build in her chest. She wanted to tell her parents, but the whole situation was so surreal, so unbelievable. They'd think she was crazy. She had to tell somebody.

Olivia picked up her phone and scrolled through her friends. She stopped on a name, her thumb hovering above it, wondering if he'd think she was crazy too. Finally, she pressed the phone icon beside his name. Luckily, he answered before she lost her nerve and hung up.

"Wassup, Ollie?"

Olivia smiled. "Uh, not much. I was just wondering if you could come over." She looked at the clock. It was past eight-thirty.

"Think your folks will spaz?" he asked.

"I'll meet you on the porch and tell them it's a school thing. Mom's had a few glasses of wine and dad is probably half asleep anyway. They won't care."

"Be there in five."

Olivia watched Rainie ditch his bike by her mailbox and walk up the short sidewalk. Smiling, he mounted the steps and joined her on the porch swing.

"Thanks for coming over."

"I'm here to serve," he said with a mock bow. "Sup? Something wrong?"

"I don't know. Maybe." Olivia took her hand off her arm and showed it to him.

"What am I looking at? Art class extra credit?"

She nudged him playfully with her elbow. "I wish. Don't think I'm crazy or anything, okay?"

Rainie shrugged. "Okay."

"Seriously, Rainie. You have to promise."

"Okay. Okay, I promise."

"The stickman, it's alive." Olivia watched his face for a reaction as he stared at the figure on her arm. She saw only incredulous disbelief.

"Alive?" he asked, looking up at her, then at the figure again. "Like, alive, alive?"

Olivia nodded. "That weirdo Julie Armistead saw it on me and said something like a spell or something in school."

She paused to judge his reaction, but still saw only disbelief in his blue eyes. "I drew it here." Olivia pointed to her wrist. "Then a rash formed, and it started moving. You see where it is now."

"Okay, let me get this straight. You drew a stickman on your wrist, Julie cast a spell on it, and it came alive?"

"Exactly. Look, I know it sounds crazy but-"

Rainie held his finger up to stop her. "It does sound crazy, Ollie. It really does. It's a doodle of a stickman."

"I know it is but listen. I drew a circle around it. See what happened?"

Rainie studied the broken circle on her arm and the bruise. "It broke out?" he asked with a grin.

"Yes, and it hurt like crazy too. Then I put this line of band-aids around my arm, hoping to catch it on one of them so I could pull it off."

"What happened?"

"I fell asleep but woke up when he pushed one of them loose and crawled under."

The boy sighed. "You do understand how this sounds, right? Is this a trick or something, Ollie?" He looked around on the porch. "Got a hidden camera or something? Am I being punked?"

"No." Olivia shook her head. "I know it sounds crazy. I tried to tell my mom and she didn't believe me either."

"Look, I'm sorry. It's just very weird, Ollie. Really. Like something off TV weird."

"I know it's weird. I know it sounds crazy. Believe me, I know." Olivia wiped a tear from her cheek. "Fine then. I'm sorry. Just go home then. I'm sorry."

"No, look. I'm sorry. Are you being for real here? No jokes or nothing?" he asked, taking her arm as she tried to turn away.

"No," she insisted. "I don't know what to do. I even tried to text Julie and she just laughed."

"What are you going to do? Have you tried washing it off?"

Olivia looked at her friend and nodded emphatically. "Yes. I've used everything I could think of. It won't come off."

Rainie took her arm and held it before him. "I wonder if we put tape on it and yanked it off."

Olivia shrugged. "Right now I'd try anything. Dad's probably got some in the garage."

Rainey tore a short piece of gray duct tape off the roll and pressed it onto Olivia's arm, covering the drawing. "It might work better if we give it a minute to transfer, or get stuck, or whatever."

The two friends stared down at the tape on Olivia's arm. "Rainie, tell me you see that." Panic was rising in Olivia's voice as she stared at her arm.

"I see it. My God, you weren't kidding," Rainie said as he stared wide-eyed at the figure wriggling beneath the tape. "Holy crap. It's like he's trying to get away."

"Okay, it's starting to burn, Rainey. Get it off."

Rainey picked at one edge of the tape, trying to raise it enough to afford him a grip.

"It's burning. C'mon. Get it off."

"I'm trying to. It's stuck pretty good."

"Get it off. It really hurts. Rainie, get it off."

Rainie finally freed a corner of the tape and snatched it free.

Olivia put a hand over her mouth to stifle a scream as she shook her arm wildly.

"Are you okay?" he asked. "Ollie?"

Olivia nodded despite the tears in her eyes. "Is it gone? I can't look."

Rainie took her arm and turned it to him. His eyes widened when he saw the figure standing in a red rectangle of a quickly growing welt. "It looks angry, somehow," he said.

"It feels angry," Ollie replied, wiping her eyes with the palm of her free hand. "What am I going to do?"

Rainie stared at her arm. "I don't know. I really don't know." He released her arm and fished his phone from his jeans pocket. "It's my mom," he said, looking at it. "I'm gonna have to go soon."

"Please don't leave me alone, Rainie. I'm starting to get scared."

"I have to. I'm just getting off being grounded from that whole thing with Kyle. They'll kill me if I stay out too late."

"Can't you tell them you're at the mall or something?"

"They know I'm here. You don't know how they are, Ollie. I'll never see the light of day again."

"What am I going to do?" she begged.

"Look," Rainie looked at her arm again, running a thumb over the red stripe where the tape had been. "Don't

55

mess with it. Maybe it won't do anything if you don't mess with it."

Olivia stared at him and shook her head. "I want it off me. I don't want it crawling around all over me."

"I know. I know. Look, leave it alone." Rainie sighed. "I'll get up early and come over. We'll figure it out tomorrow."

"Okay," she agreed reluctantly. "Thanks for coming over." Olivia shook her head as she stared down at the figure.

Rainey put a hand on her shoulder. "It's going to be okay. Just try to rest or something. You don't look so good."

"You think?" Olivia asked, pointing to her arm.

"I'm going to have to go. Look, though. I know where that psycho, Julie, lives. I'll stop by and talk to her."

"It won't help, but thanks." Olivia sighed. "Go. I don't want you to get grounded again because of me."

"I wish I could stay. I really do. That's some wild crap right there."

"Just go already."

"Okay. Text me. I'll stay up with you all night if you want."

"Thanks. Now go."

Olivia watched him leave and leaned against her father's workbench with a huff. Her eyes washed over the tools and lingered on one of the hand saws hanging on the pegboard behind the table. "Good Lord," she said shaking her head. "I'm not that desperate yet." She turned to go inside but stopped. Turning back to the table she grabbed a box cutter and slid it into her pocket before heading inside.

Sitting on her bed again, Olivia pushed the blade out of the box cutter and stared down at the stick figure. She poked it with the sharp point. It jumped suddenly, then turned to look at the blade. She poked it again, this time hard enough to draw a tiny drop of blood. The figure moved quickly to dodge the point but kicked at the blade angrily.

"You don't like that. Do ya?' she asked with a smile. "Now you know how I feel." She poked the figure again, this time catching one of the thin legs with the point of the razor. The stickman bent to the knife and grabbed his leg, trying to pull it free. When it couldn't free itself, it stood and stared up at her.

"You get off me and I won't do this again."

The stickman shook his little head slowly then turned back to the knife.

Olivia recoiled instantly as the tip of the razor began to burn, dropping the knife onto the bed.

"That's how this is gonna be?" she asked. Anger was quickly replacing the fear and desperation she'd been feeling all afternoon. "I don't know what you are, but I'm getting tired of you." Olivia jumped from her bed and rushed out the door.

As she reentered her bedroom with an ice pack, she heard her phone vibrate. Grabbing it up, she found a series of texts from Rainie.

"Went by Julie's house. Her mom wouldn't let me talk to her. Went around back."

"Her bedroom window had 10 stickmen drawn on it like the one on your arm, but bigger. They were in a line across it."

"She came to the window and flipped me off. Had to go home. Sorry. Text me."

She told him she was going to take a bath and try to sleep, then dropped the phone. Sitting on the bed, she looked at her arm again. The stickman had moved closer to her elbow, but not much. She laid the ice back on her skin, covering the figure.

After a few minutes, she removed it and stared at the stickman, its arms now folded to its chest. "Cold, little man?" she asked. The figure extended his arms and the skin around it began to warm quickly. Feeling the heat, Olivia replaced the ice pack, holding it tightly to combat the burning sensation on her skin.

The small circle of heat began to move beneath the ice pack, progressing down her arm toward her wrist.

"What the heck?" Olivia asked, gripping the ice pack. She wadded it in her hand, discovering that the frozen gel had already thawed. She shook her head. Normally the pack would have stayed cold for half an hour easily. She tossed it aside and looked at the man, now just above her wrist.

"What is your problem, dude? Just get the hell off me." She grabbed her arm next to the stickman and squeezed. "That's as far as you go."

The stickman responded by walking to her fingers and pushing against them. Tiny points of pain began, like two needles pricking her skin, but she held tight. Grimacing through the pain, she watched as he pushed harder.

"This ends now, you jerk. Do you hear me?"

The stickman drew back one hand and punched the side of her finger. Olivia gritted her teeth as she struggled to keep her hold. The stick man released a torrent of punches, each one producing a stabbing pain until Olivia finally gave up.

She shook her hand, then wiped a tear from her cheek. Olivia stared down at the man, her breath coming in angry pants. This was a violation of her body and she didn't have to stand for it. It was time to end this game.

Picking up the knife, she slid it quickly across her arm. A thin red line of blood formed on her skin that ran across the tip of the stickman's left arm. Despite the pain, a smile came to her face as she watched a section of his arm fall away.

"Now what?" she asked with a grin. "You're done, Stickie." She pulled the razor across her arm again, but the stickman hurried out of the way. She sliced at it again, but again it jumped out of the way.

"Nimble, aren't we?" she asked, her eyes narrowed as she watched the figure. She slid the knife across her arm again, this time in front of the figure. It stopped just before running into the blade and retreated. She pulled the blade across her wrist in front of it and again missed.

Olivia watched the man intently, bent over her arm as it rested in her lap. "I got you, you little bastard," she mumbled with a laugh. "I got you now."

She chased the stick figure up her arm with the knife, determined to catch him. Halfway up her forearm, she became aware of the blood running onto her lap, but only vaguely. The cuts would heal if only she could get rid of the stickman. If he would leave everything would be fine.

Just above the elbow, she almost caught him. The blade sliced through her skin, lopping off half of its right arm and a piece of his leg. The stickman turned and hobbled away from her blade, moving to the fresh, unmarked top of her arm.

"You'll not get away that easily," she said with a grin. She followed him, slicing wildly, as he ran down her arm and rounded her thumb. Cornering him in the palm of her hand, she made four quick slashes and boxed him in.

"I got you now," she said, watching as blood began to pool around the stick figure. She changed her hold on the knife and gripped it in her hand, pointing down. She stabbed at the stickman's head several times as he ducked and jumped around the tiny box of cuts.

Finally, she cornered him. He stood looking up at her defiantly next to the pool of her blood. She clenched the knife hard and drove the blade into the palm of her hand, right through the stickman's head.

She growled in pain as the blade pierced her skin but managed a satisfied smile. The stickman struggled momentarily against the blade, then fell still. Smiling, she watched as her palm filled with blood, covering the man completely.

"Okay, sweetie, I'm going to bed now. If you- oh my God!"

Olivia looked up to find her mother running toward her.

"What have you done? Frank! Frank!" She wrestled the knife from her daughter and threw it across the room just as her husband entered.

"It's over," Olivia said with a smile as her mother hugged her. "It's okay now, mom. I fixed it."

The doctor adjusted his glasses and looked at the worried couple sitting before him. "I'm not going to sugarcoat this. Your daughter is deeply disturbed emotionally. This wasn't a textbook suicide attempt, but it was a textbook cry for help. One is as bad as the other. Olivia has some very deep-seated emotional issues."

"But she was fine. She's been fine. Good grades, friends. Everything."

"Mister Hayden, I can't tell you how many parents have sat in that same chair and said the same thing. What we think we know and what we actually know is often rather dissimilar."

"She did not try to kill herself!"

"Maybe, maybe not. Either way, she cut herself one hundred and four times. That is not typical behavior."

"What's this stickman she keeps talking about? What is that?"

"It's a deflection, an excuse. She doesn't want to face whatever is bothering her or admit that she hurt herself because of it. I've heard all sorts of excuses."

"But I did see a stickman doodle on her wrist. The nurse bandaged the rash that formed around it."

"I believe there may have been something, but I feel like the rash was just the beginning of this episode. She probably did it herself, the rash I mean. All of this isn't new.

61

Believe me." The doctor clasped his hands before him and sighed. "But we've searched her from head to toe and didn't find anything. Short of shaving her head, we saw no stickman. Believe me, when I tell you, it's not about the figure she drew on herself. This is a much deeper issue."

"What do we do now?" Frank Hayden slid forward in his chair. "Can we fix her?"

The doctor shook his head. "It's not about 'fixing' her, but rather healing her. And to do that I'm recommending you commit her for a while. Thirty days at the very least."

"Thirty days?" Brenda asked as tears began to roll down her cheeks.

"At least. She's a very disturbed little girl."

Olivia sat on her hospital bed, slowly unraveling the fresh bandages from her left arm. With each revolution of the bloody wrap, she examined her skin carefully. She methodically made her way down her arm to the wrist, satisfied that the stickman was gone. Pulling the gauze from her wrist and hand, she examined the fresh wounds carefully.

Nodding her head, she smiled. She scratched the right side of her head as she laid back on the bed, staring up at the plain white ceiling. It was over. She had won.

Closing her eyes, she relaxed into the pillow with a heavy sigh.

Yawning, she raised a hand and scratched her head through her long blonde hair. She wanted a shower almost as much as she wanted to sleep. Friday morning felt like a lifetime ago. Between school, battling the stickman, the doctors at the Emergency Room, and being brought here, she'd been awake for most of the past thirty-six hours and her body was begging for relief.

Raising a hand again, she scratched her head just above her right ear, wondering what was making her head itch so bad.

Olivia Hayden's eyes flew open suddenly as both hands went to her hair. Her screams echoed in the closed rooms as her hands closed around two fistfuls of hair and began to pull.

The Secret Life of Robert Freely

Amanda Freely awoke with a start from her doze on the couch. Her eyes scanned the living room, then came to rest on the door to the basement. The source of the noise that woke her was beyond the door. Pulling the terrycloth robe tighter around her neck, she began to wonder if the basement door leading to the backyard was locked. She never went down there. It always smelled damp and musty and although it was partially finished, the lighting was bad. It was her husband's domain and she only traversed the steps if she had to.

Her heart began to race when she heard sounds of movement. A quick look at the clock on the wall told her it was three in the morning. It was both too late and too early for anyone to be up to anything good.

She waited patiently, following the sounds from the basement as they moved about. Her brow furrowed momentarily when she heard the sound of a shower running, but then she nodded. Her suspicions were right on the mark.

The person in the basement was Robert, her husband. For months now, she'd had her suspicions about him. So many times he'd gotten out of their bed and crept down to the basement, then out the door. After a few hours, he would always return, sometimes showering, sometimes not. He'd then change back into his pajamas and sneak back into bed.

Of course, she pretended to be asleep, not wanting a confrontation in the middle of the night. He was a good husband, a good man, and she believed with all her heart that he would be a great father. If they were able to have kids, that is. For twenty years he'd always treated her well, gone out of his way to make her feel loved and appreciated. He'd even been a champ throughout her breast cancer scare. When she needed someone, he was always there.

He worked very hard for long hours to build the life they enjoyed now and only last year made vice president of State Bank, the fourth-largest bank in Alabama. He made very good money, which allowed her the freedom to not work, yet he still insisted on hiring a maid to help her out around the house.

Amanda sighed. They had a good life. Was she willing to throw it all away over a few nocturnal dalliances? Robert was an important man under lots of stress. So what if he needed an outlet? Everybody had their vices. Some men drank, some men gambled, some men beat the hell out of their wives. Nobody was perfect.

Rubbing her eyes, Amanda scolded herself for making excuses for him. What he was doing was wrong and she should be angry. She should be shocked, or dismayed, or at least perturbed, but she wasn't. It was a truth she'd accepted some time ago.

There was a secret part of her that liked the idea. There was a small part that she kept hidden from her friends at the country club that enjoyed it. Knowing his secret was powerful, but that wasn't the only thing she liked. There was a certain virility to it that made her heart flutter with excitement. She'd never expected her docile, well-mannered husband capable of such things. As bad as she hated to admit it, it turned her on a little. It wasn't normal, but it was true. It was the "manliest" thing she'd ever known him to do. Robert didn't hunt or fish watched very little sports and only golfed when his position required it of him. He didn't smoke or drink and rarely ever used foul language. Robert Freely was a regular boy scout. Most of the time.

His "adventures" weren't frequent, and they didn't cost them much money. It wasn't like he kept a whore in a personal apartment somewhere. Why should she begrudge him the opportunity to blow off some steam every now and then? Especially when it improved their marriage.

For weeks after his nights out, Robert would be a doting husband. He would attend to her every need, in and out of the bedroom. He would buy her flowers and gifts. They would go out to nice restaurants. At first, she figured it was guilt, but now she realized that it was his real nature. It was the Robert she dated in college, the Robert she'd fallen in love with.

After a few weeks, when the stress and aggravation of his job slowly began to build, he would morph back into the bitter, self-loathing man she had grown used to. As the glow of his nighttime excursion began to fade, he too would fade into the businessman, then the banker, then the middle-aged man with thinning hair, full of silent rage and resentment. His job was killing him. Was he so wrong to seek a quick respite now and then?

She imagined him coming home, suit coat unbuttoned, briefcase in hand. He would be irritable and grumpy and tired. Mentally tired. He would eat supper with her, put on a brave face, and pretend he was fine, but she knew he wasn't. He hated his job. It had turned into a monster that he continually had to feed and when he didn't feed it, it ate a part of him.

Amanda crossed her legs, pulling the robe over her knee as she straightened herself on the couch. Robert was coming up the steps now. She'd rehearsed this moment many times and knew that she had to be careful not to overplay her hand. Tonight would be a pivotal night in their marriage. Tonight would change everything.

Detective Randall Coats walked out of the suburban home of Joe and Emily Bancroft and stood on the front porch. His eyes scanned the line of police tape surrounding the yard, illuminated every few seconds by the flashing light of the patrol cars that lined the street. Another crime scene. Two more murders. Another sleepless night.

He lit a cigarette and inhaled deeply before descending the steps to the sidewalk where his Lieutenant awaited him.

"I thought you quit."

"I did," Coats replied dryly. He took another draw off the cigarette and blew the smoke skyward. "Six times I quit, six times I started back. Can't seem to kick 'em."

"After this, I might need a smoke."

Coats looked back through the open door of the house and shook his head. "I'll never get used to this shit, Bennie."

"I hope you never do."

Coats looked at his lieutenant. "Same pattern as before, only worse. It's definitely our guy."

Bennie sighed. "That's six times in three years. Twelve dead."

"Yep." Coats took another draw and dropped the cigarette to the sidewalk, smashing it with his foot before picking up the butt. "And let me guess, nobody saw anything."

"Not so far. Uniforms are canvassing the neighborhood."

"How does it happen here?" Coats asked, looking around. "This isn't New York or L.A."

"Crazy people are everywhere, my friend."

"Guesso." Coats ran a hand across the stubble that covered his cheeks. "It just doesn't make sense. The brutality, the anger. It's almost like he hates his victims."

"Maybe he does."

"There's been nothing to connect any of the other murders. There is no common denominator. We've been through everyone in their lives with a fine-tooth comb."

"Maybe he hates everybody."

"How the hell can that be random?" Coats jerked a thumb toward the house while his other hand fished the half-empty pack of Marlboros from his shirt pocket. He had five more years before he could retire with a full pension, but he knew if he ever caught this guy he'd be done. He'd stay if it took ten, but he'd leave if they caught him next week.

The detective lit another cigarette and took a deep draw on it.

"It amazes me that one human being can be so...." he searched for a word. "So depraved. I mean, what the hell does this guy think about all day? What reason could you possibly have for doing that to anyone, let alone a stranger?" He blew smoke toward the open door and shook his head again. This guy was getting under his skin and he couldn't help it. He wanted to catch him because it was his job and to save lives, but he also just wanted to see what the maniac looked like, how he lived.

He always imagined him in some crummy one-bedroom apartment, dirty, smoking pot and watching cartoons while flies darted around a bare light bulb hanging over his head. Nothing at any of the scenes lent him that notion, but his mind had conjured it early in the investigation and it had stuck.

"Does there have to be a reason? We're obviously dealing with a sick person here, Coats."

Coats shrugged, trying to clear it of the images he'd just seen. Just like the other crime scenes, this one was strewn with blood. The bodies were naked, stabbed multiple times. The only differences were how each victim was killed. Sometimes the man was stabbed to death, sometimes the wife was stabbed to death. Whichever one didn't die by the knife was strangled after being bound and gagged. Both men and women would be naked, but neither showed any signs of sexual aggression.

"Why do you think he goes back and forth stabbing the husband or the wife?" Coats asked.

"Hell if I know."

"They usually don't do that. It's odd." Coats rubbed his mouth. "Look, do you think it could be a copycat?"

"What? Two serial killers in our little town? Na. Statistically, that's nearly impossible. It's one guy. They're zeroing in on a profile."

"It just doesn't make sense," Coats persisted. "Why switch back and forth?"

"When does stabbing someone ten times ever make sense? It's a psychopath, Coats. Just go where the evidence leads you."

The detective opened his mouth to protest but closed it without saying a word. He shook his head and looked back at the open doorway.

"The M.E. is on his way."

"Easy one for him. Cause of death, multiple stab wounds to the chest and torso, just like the others." Coats blew smoke over his shoulder.

"Crime scene analysis is coming too. Let's clear everyone out of the area."

"Sometimes I hate this job," Coats mumbled, more to himself than anyone else.

"I do too, buddy. But what else are we gonna do? We're cops."

"I could have been a butcher," Coats answered. "There'd be less blood."

"Have a nice night?"

The color drained from Robert's face as he stood in the basement doorway still clutching the knob in his left hand.

"Uh-you're-uh-up. Why are you up?"

"Surprised?"

"Uh-yes." He closed the door. "I guess so. I was-uh-in the basement. Couldn't sleep. I mean, I couldn't sleep so I went to the basement."

"The basement?" Amanda asked, one eyebrow slightly arched.

"Yeah," Robert replied with a nervous smile as he began to gather himself after the shock of seeing his wife. "Just tinkering. Did I wake you?"

"No, Robert. You didn't wake me because you weren't in the basement."

"I just came from there." He jerked a thumb at the door behind him.

"I know you went to the basement. But I also know you didn't stay in the basement."

Robert let out a forced laugh. "Whatever do you mean, sweetie. Of course, I was in the basement."

"Robert, Robert, Robert," she sighed. "I know your secrets. I know you snuck out." Amanda stood and crossed the room. "And I know this isn't the first time you've done it."

"I don't know what you're talking about, love. That's ridiculous."

Amanda put a finger to his lips. "Do not lie to me, Robert. I know what you've been up to." Amanda leveled her gaze at her husband. "I know what dirty little things you've been doing."

Robert shrunk under her gaze. "Look, Mandy, I can explain," he began, panic rising into his eyes. "It's not what you think."

"Oh, I think it is." Amanda put a finger under his chin and led him to the couch. "Sit down and let me see if I got this right."

Robert complied and started to defend himself, but she stopped him.

"I have been keeping a diary, Robert. I know dates, times, everything. I also read the newspaper, my dear. So when I say I know about your dirty little playthings, believe me. I know everything."

"I-I don't know what to say."

Amanda smiled. Her hands went to the knot holding her robe together and slowly untied it. She slid it over her shoulders and dropped it to the floor. She smiled again, enjoying the look of shocked confusion on his face.

She pushed his knees together and crawled onto his lap. "Tell me everything," she whispered seductively as her lips touched his neck. "I want to know all the details."

"What? You're not making sense."

"Oh, Robert. You know exactly what I'm talking about. I know you've seen all the papers and the news. You know exactly what I'm talking about." She leaned in and kissed him, letting her tongue linger on his lips. "We've got to decide on something tonight, my dear."

"What?" he asked, still confused by her reaction.

Amanda Freely looked at her husband and smiled. "We've got to decide who the copycat is."

The Incident at Bitterweed Creek

When Bitterweed Creek began its annual rise, not many people paid much attention. It had been a wet spring and the river that it fed was up so there was nowhere for it to go. As more rain fell and the river got higher and the creek got deeper, a few people began to cast wary eyes toward it.

I first noticed this one afternoon while riding my bike after school. There were quite a few of us from families that couldn't afford to buy another car just because we turned sixteen. For us, riding bikes as teenagers simply felt like a continuation of what we'd been doing our whole lives. Besides, the town was small and any friend I might want to visit didn't live more than a mile or two from me anyway.

I saw an old man standing on the bridge on Washington Street, just staring at the muddy water below. Coming closer, I saw it was Lester Anderson, one of the oldest men in town. I rolled up and greeted him politely, but he just looked at me, shook his head, and shuffled away.

It was a peculiar incident that piqued my teenage mind enough to make me pay more attention to the otherwise overlooked senior crowd in town. They could easily be found sitting in groups at the diner drinking coffee or on each other's porches, also drinking coffee. Sometimes they would hurl an admonition the way of us younger folks, but we were usually already past them when they did so, so it fell on deaf ears.

On that same evening, my own grandfather spent what I considered an inordinate length of time staring out the window, watching the rain collect in muddy puddles in our driveway. I asked him if he was okay. He looked at me with a grim smile, nodded, and hobbled off, no doubt feeling the effects of arthritis in his hip.

That night a storm rolled through and dumped another inch of rain on our already water-logged town and more people began to worry about Bitterweed Creek, most of whom were the fathers of our fathers. It might have been easy to dismiss as the habit of old men to worry about the weather, if not for the peculiar activity of the old folks.

Groups of them began to pop up around town. Sometimes there were three or four, sometimes more. Often, the same grandfathers could be seen in different groups throughout that wet Saturday in March. It might have been comical, if not so peculiar. They looked like us teenagers, only older and there was no laughing or messing around. And we didn't drink coffee.

I grabbed my mom's umbrella and headed to Washington Street to see what all the fuss was about. It was the only place in town where Bitterweed Creek passed beneath a road. The rest of the creek meandered along the edge of town, bordering various cow pastures, hayfields, and most of a large farm belonging to Rutherford Simmons before disappearing into the woods and continuing south where it emptied into the Alabama River.

When I got there, the first thing I noticed was that the normally docile creek where I'd spent many hot, summer days splashing around and catching crawfish, was a torrent of dark brown water swelled well past its banks. The second thing was the suspicious looks I was getting from the three old men standing on the bridge. I recognized one of them as my friend Tommy's grandfather. I couldn't place the other two despite seeing them countless times around town.

"What are you doing here?" one of the strangers asked me in a gruff voice possessed by so many old men.

"Same as you, I suspect. Looking at the creek."

"Well you saw it, now run along."

I looked at the old men for a moment and saw worry in their eyes, righteous indignation, and maybe a little fear, but I couldn't be sure about the last one. They looked nervous about something and it had to do with the creek.

"You know, the creek's never flooded the town before," I told them.

"You don't know everything, young man. You don't even know what you think you know. Now run along."

I turned my bike around and rode away slowly, sparing them a look over my shoulder. After I left, the three men went back to the conversation they'd been having before I rode up.

Long after supper that night, somewhere close to nine o'clock, my mother woke her father up to take a phone call that came in on the mostly dormant landline. As he did most nights after supper, he'd fallen asleep in the recliner in the living room. She stretched the cord and sat the phone on his chair-side table and handed him the receiver. He mostly listened, nodded a few times, and finally gave the caller an "Okay" before thanking him for calling and hanging up.

He pushed himself out of the chair with a grunt and went to the window. He let out a low moan as he watched more rainfall into the ever-growing puddle that was quickly consuming our driveway.

A lot of men skipped church the next day, but no one was surprised. It was a cold, wet morning in mid-March, and getting out of a warm bed to hear a long-winded preacher wasn't very appetizing to me either. My mother, however, was determined that the Lord was going to see me through my vulnerable teenage years, so she and I went alone. Her power of persuasion was less effective on my father, so he stayed home.

As the preacher droned on about some guy killing a bunch of folks with the jawbone of an ass, a topic that would normally draw at least a few adolescent giggles from me, I noticed that not one single elder was present. Not even Brother Simmons, normally a fixture of the third-row aisle seat on the right side. Aside from an occasional trip into town for necessities, the only reason he left his property was for church.

It might have been the weather, but I remember many Sunday mornings when the preacher only had my mother, myself, Brother Simmons, and a few members of the choir to preach to. His absence was conspicuous, to say the least.

One of the things that always amazed me about being in church was how encompassing it was. The world was still going on outside, you just didn't know about it. You sat in the pew, listened to the preacher and the choir and it felt like time stopped. But it didn't. Things were happening outside, sometimes important things. That's exactly how it was on that particular Sunday morning.

When we were finally released from the bubble of Beulah Baptist Church, we discovered that the town was abuzz with the news that Brother Simmons' lower field had flooded in the night. It came as no surprise to me. The field in question was a low, flat area that jutted out into the creek's path, forming a horseshoe bend. Even in the driest springs, it was always the last area to be plowed because it often stayed wet, as evidenced by the healthy crop of wild ferns and moss that lined the creek in that area.

There was also a peculiar shaped Alder tree there. A dozen or so twisted, gnarly shoots had sprung up from the stump of what had to have been a large tree felled many years ago. The new shoots had interwoven themselves at odd angles, more closely resembling a giant briar patch than the normally majestic Alder.

It seemed much ado about nothing to me since the crops planted in that field never did well anyway.

By midafternoon, the bridge on Washington Street was the focus of many of the townsfolk, except the notable exception of old men. People came down and watched the water go by, made bad jokes or their own predictions about the water level, then went about their way, happy for an afternoon without rain. No one seemed to miss the old guys at all. Except me.

I was lost in thought on the suspicious behavior of the town's elder members when I heard someone say, "What the heck is that?"

I looked up to see a wooden box bobbing in the water upstream about fifty or sixty yards. Standing near the center of the old concrete bridge, I had a near-perfect view into the tunnel created by the canopy of trees that hung over the creek.

Waterlogged and heavy, it caught on some tree roots for a moment, then the churning water dislodged it and brought it toward us. Someone suggested getting a rope and the crowd erupted in movement.

Most of us moved in a wave to one side of the bridge or the other, casting our lots onto the side each of us thought it might come closer to. We clambered down the muddy embankments as far more excitement than should have climbed into our minds.

Those on my side, standing on a sandy flat that lead down to the water's edge, stared at those on the other side, sloshing through mud and pushing through cattail shoots still green and firm.

The underside of the bridge, being foreign to many of the townsfolk, gathered some attention. Somewhere I knew that there would be talk of the graffiti at a later date, but it wouldn't be today. Today most of us were fixated on the box as it slowly made its way along the bank that I was situated on.

Some of my fellow east bankers might have chosen this side by sheer luck or proximity, but I had a good familiarity with the underside of the Washington Street bridge. I'd fished, swam, and even spent some time holding a can of spray paint beneath that bridge. It was where I'd taken my first, and last puffs off a Marlboro Red, and where I'd kissed Missy Spencer when we were both ten.

Mister Henson, the father of a girl I dated briefly in eighth grade, showed up with a rope and tossed it the twenty-odd feet across the muddy water to a man on the other side. They both went to the water's edge and held the rope taut just above the surface while most of the others offered advice as if they'd wrangled many boxes from a raging torrent of water before.

I stood silently and watched. Only mildly curious while everyone else was enraptured with the possibilities of what the box might contain, I noticed something they did not. An old brown truck, its age well past mine, stopped on the bridge momentarily then pulled away in a hurry. I just caught a glimpse of the gray-haired man driving it, but it was enough to tell me that Brother Simmons' normally pale face was ghostly white. His eyes caught mine for a brief instant, but in that instant, I realized that whatever was in that box wasn't meant to be found.

I went to the water's edge and took up a position behind Mister Henson, suddenly determined to find out what was in that box. He spared me a glance, then turned his attention back to the rapidly approaching prize.

As it floated closer, I could tell the box was bigger than it appeared. I wiped my hands on my khakis, which were already dirty enough to draw my mother's ire, and gripped the rope tighter. With the water behind it, the box was going to be hard to stop.

The box bobbed in the water as it entered the shade of the bridge. Hitting the stanchion on my side, it spun around and skittered on the rocky bottom before the water pushed it along its course. Mister Henson told everyone to get ready and we all stiffened our backs against the expected weight of the oncoming box.

It caught on the rope about three inches down from the top and hung there for a moment. The rushing water pushed against it, causing the rope to bow slightly, but we held tight. A collective gasp went up from the crowd as the box tilted backward, its bottom pushed by the water. Someone shouted for another rope, but no one left to get one.

"Listen, Charlie," Mister Henson shouted in his deep, authoritative voice, "I'm gonna feed slack on my side while y'all hold tight. The water should push it closer to the edge over here. Okay?"

Charlie agreed and the men put the plan into action. Me and Mister Henson slowly worked our way down the muddy bank, watching the box carefully. When the box slid toward our bank the crowd cheered as if we'd all won something. When the box hung a snag, they fell quiet again.

We offered slack and the water pushed the box closer to us, then repeated the motion two more times until the box sat on the mud just off the bank. Unwilling to get his shoes wet, Mister Henson suggested I retrieve the box.

A shiver ran through me as my bare foot disappeared beneath the cold water. Mud on the bottom squished between my toes with each step as I inched away from the bank, beyond the depth of my rolled-up church pants. I knew my mother wouldn't be happy with me, but I was in too deep to turn back now, both figuratively and literally.

When my hand first grasped the slimy, dark surface of the box I jerked it away, sure that I had been shocked. I looked around, expecting to see a lot of surprised faces, but no one had noticed. Instead, they were encouraging me. I reached out again, more tentatively this time but felt only the punky wood of the box and the slime that only comes from being wet for a long time. I grasped it with both hands and wrestled it toward the bank. When I got it close enough, several men helped haul it out of the water while I put my socks and shoes back on.

It was well-made, with reinforcing boards at the edges, and now sat encircled by an ever-growing crowd, like a football trophy. Measuring roughly four feet by two feet and colored by the Alabama mud, it looked out of place in the sunshine that had finally broken through the clouds.

Someone in the back of the crowd suggested that it was old enough to contain buried treasure, but everyone ignored him as Mister Henson approached the box. He took out his pocketknife and scraped some of the sludge from the top. "It's Alder wood", he proclaimed. "Probably why it didn't rot."

"Hell, let's bust it open and see what's inside." James Inglewood, my former P.E. teacher, and baseball coach stepped forward with a hammer and pry bar.

Above us on the road, tires slid to a stop and men began filing out of trucks. "Don't touch that box." The gruff voice rolled over the crowd like a fog, garnering everyone's attention. All eyes shifted from the box to the collection of old men making their way down the embankment, led by David Xavier. The third man in line was my grandfather. The worried look that had become a mainstay on his face had changed to something that bordered on panic.

This couldn't be good.

Mr. Inglewood asked them, "Why the hell not?"

"Because it's my property," Brother Simmons replied as he made the landing where we were. Several people moved quickly to surround their hard-earned prize and to cut him off from reaching it.

"We fished it out the creek," someone in back insisted. "Ain't yours no more."

"It's mine and we come to take it back. The floodwaters washed it off my property, but it's still mine."

"I beg to differ, Brother Simmons. It was in the creek. There's nothing that says you own it but you."

"Ain't that good enough?"

"Not for me," someone shouted from the back. "What's in it?"

"Nobody's business what's in it. It's mine and I'll be taking it." The group of a dozen or so old men tightened into a knot and took a step forward. The crowd surrounding the box did the same.

"What's in the box, Simmons?" Mister Henson asked.

"None of yer damned business! It's mine and I'm taking it home." He pushed forward but was stopped by the younger, stronger hand of James Inglewood.

"Nobody's doing nothing of the sort. If it's yours, prove it or you might wanna get the sheriff because we're opening it."

The old men all protested, but David Xavier's voice was the loudest. "You're a damned fool, James. Always have been."

He looked at the old man and shrugged. "Don't change nothing."

The old men, not used to having their word questioned, whether out of reverence or simple politeness, stared at the faces staring back at them. They were outnumbered by a younger, stronger crowd that wanted the box opened. Their chances of getting the box were waning, then my grandfather stepped forward.

"Look, folks, this is Brother Simmons' box. I can testify to it, and so can most all the men here." He spoke solemnly as his eyes swept over the crowd. "It was buried in his low field a long time ago before most of y'all were even born. What's in it ain't no concern to anyone but him and us."

"So what the hell's in it?"

"It doesn't matter. Believe me when I tell y'all you don't wanna know. It's personal. Leave it be."

"I don't believe you, old man!" someone shouted from the back.

I looked around to see who had yelled at my grandfather, but whoever it was had melted back into the crowd before I could identify them.

"Pawpaw, why can't you tell us?" I asked, stepping forward. When he looked at me, I saw a profound sadness in his eyes and a determination that I hadn't seen in a long time.

"I can't, son. That should be enough."

My resolve weakened under his gaze and I slumped back a few steps, deflated. He was my father's father. I'd never not minded his word and wouldn't start today.

Rutherford Simmons took a deep breath and exhaled slowly as his expression changed from anger to sadness. Following his gaze, the crowd parted enough for him to see the box. When his eyes fell on it for the first time in nearly seventy years, he shook his head.

Moving slowly, he made his way through the crowd. When he laid a hand on the box and began to weep quietly, the crowd moved back a step, collectively realizing that something had suddenly changed.

"Y'all want to know what's in the box?" he asked, his voice a hoarse whisper.

The murmur of a guilty yes came from the crowd like the last air escaping a balloon.

"Brother Simmons, you're upset. Let's go home." My grandfather put a hand on his shoulder.

"Yeah. Y'all have done this to an old man. Proud of yourselves?" David Xavier glared at the crowd. "Damned fools."

"Stop it." Simmons shrugged his friend's hand off his shoulder and turned to look at the men he'd arrived with.

"I'm tired of it all. Tired of living like this. It wasn't y'all who had to live alone all these years. It wasn't y'all who lived with this."

"Look, Brother Simmons, we all know what you're going through."

"Do ya!" Simmons looked at the group of old men and shook his head. "I don't reckon you have any idea."

David Xavier stepped close to Simmons and leaned in close to him. "Don't be stupid. We all knew what we was a-doin'. Don't forget that. You was there too. You're as guilty as the rest of us."

"Some might say you was to blame," my grandfather added.

Rutherford Simmons looked at both men with such a vile disdain that the crowd took another step back, sensing trouble. With what little strength his spindly arms could muster, he pushed David in the chest, staggering him momentarily.

"I hope you burn in the pits of hell, you piece of crap you. What are you going to do? The buzzards have come home to roost and there ain't nothing any of y'all can do about it now."

I looked at my grandfather after he spoke to Simmons, but he dropped his gaze and turned away, rejoining the group at the bottom of the hill. Looking at the collection of men, I saw the history of the town. I saw church elders, town leaders, businessmen, and other men of distinction.

The pillars of the town were weakening under the strain of whatever was in that box and looked ready to collapse, their faces suddenly gaunt and aged beyond their years. I saw my past, and in Rutherford Simmons, they saw theirs, resurfaced after so many years just like the old wooden box.

To me, the men looked like they'd seen a ghost.

In the brief few seconds that the two men stared at each other; I saw something new in each of their eyes. In Mr. Simmons, I saw righteous anger and intensity that matched any I'd ever seen before. In Mr. Xavier, I saw a shame that had never been there. I also saw something I couldn't understand then but would come to know as relief. Whatever was in that box had been a mighty burden on him, and probably the rest of the men as well.

"It's too late to tell tales now, Rutherford. You just going to hurt more people than's already been hurt."

"Let the man talk," James said, now standing in defense of the old man. "I wanna hear it."

The crowd began murmuring for more information.

Simmons looked up at David and shook his head. "I'm done hiding it, being quiet. I don't wanna go to my grave with this. I'm going to do what I ought to have done years ago."

David Xavier opened his mouth to protest but closed it. He shook a finger at Rutherford Simmons as he struggled for something to say, but just threw his hand at him in a dismissive wave when nothing came to him. Lowering his head, he walked through the crowd of his contemporaries and climbed the hill to his truck.

When Brother Simmons began to talk the other old men each left one by one. Some got into their cars, some just made their way home on foot. They all knew what he was going to say and didn't want to face it.

"I was a young man when the travelin' show stopped out the train station. Weren't much here back then 'cept the train station, cotton fields, and a whole lotta kids to work in 'em, so we all went out to see it. We was all there when she walked down those steps of the train. I reckon everybody's jaw dropped as far as mine. She was the prettiest thing I ever saw; anybody ever saw probably. Long hair as black as soot and shiny as glass, green eyes, and a smile that went on for days. We was falling over ourselves to talk to her, but she never paid nobody no mind, but me. I don't rightly know why. I wasn't the biggest, or strongest, or even the best looking, but I was sure glad she did.

"They set up a camp down by the tracks at the edge of town. Her daddy performed magic tricks and juggled things like knives and fire sticks and the like. It was amazing to watch him, but he wasn't the one I came to see. Sophia wore this fancy dress and was his assistant."

"Every night, after the show was over, I stayed and helped put things away just to talk to her. Sophia Magladoni was her name. As hard as it was to believe, she was just a regular girl. We talked almost all night about nothing, or maybe everything. She had a laugh." He shook his head as a smile tugged at the corners of his mouth. "A laugh that could melt a boy's heart. And it did. I don't know about her, but I was head over heels in love."

Every time I'd ever seen Rutherford Simmons before that day his face was a mask of loneliness, which made the sparkle that appeared in his eyes and the smile on his thin lips even more surprising. What I'd always taken for sternness was sadness, for disdain was heartbreak.

He was old and had never married. People said he worked his farm all day and went to bed early, only to do the same the next day. I'd always just assumed him a miser, like most of the other old men born to parents who had weathered the great depression. The truth was that I'd made a great many assumptions about the people of this town, and the knot in my stomach told me I was wrong about a lot of them. Especially the old men.

As he continued talking the twinkle faded and so did my smile. "Well, word got out that we was talking and some of the boys were powerful jealous. It was like they hated me because I was talking to her. Some of them called her names and made fun of her family because they were from "the old country". I don't know what that meant, but I knew they would have given anything to be in my shoes, so it didn't bother me none.

Some of the boys got together and hatched a plan though. It was powerful hot that summer and the plan was to talk her into coming swimming at the creek behind our place. The boys were going to hide in the bushes and watch when she changed into her bathing suit so they could see her naked."

The old man shook his head and ran a hand along the top of the box with a heavy sigh.

"I didn't like the idea, but I was a scrawny thing back then and some of the boys used their fists to persuade me to go along. The whole time, I knew it wasn't right and I felt bad for ever going along with it. But I guess a part of me was scared, and another part of me wanted to be part of the gang.

"I don't know how it happened, but we ended up swimming. Skinny dipping I guess you call it. When she come out from behind those bushes without a stitch of clothes on I nearly fainted. My heart stopped beating for a few minutes and I must have looked a sight. I remember she laughed. It wasn't a mean laugh but like a nervous laugh. Or maybe she was laughing at the expression on my face. I don't know.

"I reckon the boys got more than they bargained for. I guess I did too. I was a young man and she was a young girl and we were there in our nakedness before God and everybody else. Things happened that come natural to young folks I suppose, and the other boys saw it all."

The old man paused and took several weak breaths as a grimace appeared suddenly on his face. Someone helped him to the box so that he might lean against it.

"I don't know if it drove them all crazy or if they were jealous, or what, but they all came out of the bushes and just stared at us. When I saw 'em all on the banks I knew there would be trouble. I could see it in their eyes. I told Sophia to run, but it was no use. They was like a pack of wolves.

"Half of 'em lit in on me and started punching and kicking me. Now, my daddy was a big man and he laid some whoopins on me but none of 'em ever hurt like that did. Most everybody wore boots of some kind of other back then and a swift kick in the ribs was a powerful thing to take. And I took plenty.

"The other half of the boys lit in on her. I reckon she'd have rather they beat her too, 'cause she fought 'em something fierce. I know she got some good licks in on a few of them and I was glad she did. More than one of them left there bleeding."

Simmons lowered his gaze to the box, unable to look at the crowd, now hanging on his every word.

"All the boys had her, most of 'em more than once. Wasn't nothing I could do to stop 'em. Every time I tried to get up, I got kicked or punched back down. I lost nearly half my teeth in that field and a whole lot of blood too. It was way yonder after dark when the last of 'em finished with her and left us alone."

"I crawled to her and tried to help, but it was too late." He began to weep again as the years of pent-up emotion boiled over. "Even after all that, all that they'd done to her, she was still beautiful. I brushed the hair from her face and told her I was sorry. So sorry. I don't know if she could hear me or not. I hope she did.

"There weren't nothing I could do. She was gone. I took her torn up dress and covered her up best I could. I couldn't leave her like that. Took me nearly three hours to crawl home from that lower field. When I made it home, I told Mama what happened, then I reckon I passed out."

Simmons raised a trembling hand to his chest and bent forward slightly. Two men rushed in to support him, but he pushed them away.

"When I woke up people had been talking to my folks. Every one of them boys got their story straight and every one of 'em lied. I don't know if my daddy believed them or me, or if he just wanted it done with. He told me he took that Alder wood he had milled for the new church communion table and make a casket to bury the girl in. I've never seen it before today." He looked at the box and shook his head.

"He buried her down there where it all happened. He said it won't do any good to talk to the sheriff 'cause one of his boys was in the group. He said what happened could ruin one life or a dozen lives and it was best not to talk about it again."

The people closed on the weakening man, quietly offering sympathies. An undercurrent of righteous anger was beginning to flow through the crowd. I hoped things wouldn't get out of hand and wished they would at the same time.

"I don't deserve no relief," he said, shaking his head slowly. "I should've spoke up years ago. I should've gone to her folks and told 'em where she was, but they'd already left town. So many years I've thought of them wondering where she went and what happened to her." He sighed and wiped a tear from his strained face as he stared down at the box.

"So many years she's been down in that box, our secret buried with her. So many years." Brother Simmons leaned forward as his knees buckled. His frail body fell on the box and slipped to the ground before anyone could grab him.

He quieted the crowd with a weak wave of his hand as Fran Young, a plump woman who ran the register at the diner, raised him to her lap. "We got a family plot out to my place. It's on a hill. There's sunshine and wildflowers there. I think she'd like it." The old man grimaced in pain as a hand went to his chest again.

When the pain eased, he looked up at the faces staring down at him. In the distance, an ambulance siren wailed, but the look on his face said he knew he was too far gone.

"She didn't deserve what happened. I don't suppose I did either. I spent all these years praying for forgiveness, but I don't know if I got it or not. I know this is a coward's way, saying all this here at the end, and I guess you'd be right if you said so. I wrote everything down, all the names and what they did. They's evil in the hearts of those men, no matter how long they been keeping it hid. Y'all can decide what to do about it now. I got a safe deposit box down the bank. It's in there."

The ambulance arrived with a patrol car in tow. Mister Henson met the Police Chief at his car.

"Scott, you better call Mister Anderson down at the bank. He's gonna have to open up. And you might want to call Barney Grimes too. I think all hell is about to break loose."

"What in the world is going on? What's happened? What are all those people doing?"

"Simmons' lower field has flooded, and something's come unearthed. That box down there, I don't know what the hell is in it, but I think it's big. I'll explain everything on the way. Trust me, you're going to want to read what's in Simmons' safety deposit box."

"Can't it wait 'till the morning? Hell, it's Sunday afternoon."

"No, Scott. It can't. Too many years have been wasted already."

"You ain't making no sense, Carl. Stop acting a damned fool and tell me what's happened. Start with who the ambulance is for."

"Mr. Simmons had a heart attack. I think he's dead or close to it. Anyways, the ambulance is for him. It's all about that box we fished outta the creek. A bunch of old guys, David Xavier, Robert McCloud, and some others showed up and wanted the box. We said we fished it out of the creek and were going to open it. They got real mad and there was almost a fight, 'till Simmons stepped in."

The chief looked over Carl Henson's shoulder as the paramedics lifted the stretcher into the back of the ambulance. "He going to be alright?"

"I don't think so."

"Damn. Always liked him." He looked at the mob of people still gathered around the box and pushed past Carl Henson. "Nobody touches that box," he said, surveying the group on the landing below him. "It's in police custody for now. Anybody even lay a finger on it and I'll run you in. Be best if everyone just went home." He stared at the crowd, but nobody moved.

"Now, Carl, tell me what in the hell happened."

"I told you. We fished that box outta the creek. The old guys showed up and got mad because we were going to open it. They said it washed off Rutherford Simmons' lower field because of the flood. They wanted it, but we wouldn't give it up. That's when Simmons showed up and started talking." He rubbed the back of his neck. "Is it or is it not public property if it's in the creek? 'Cause I want to open it."

"We ain't in elementary school, Carl. It's not finders keepers. Shit. What did Simmons say?"

Carl Henson grabbed the sheriff's arm and looked him in the eye. "He said there was a rape and a murder a long time ago when they all was boys. Some girl from a traveling show." He put a hand on the Chief's shoulder. "Scott, I think her body is in that box."

"What in the holy hell?" he asked, his eyes going to the box. "It doesn't look like a casket."

"Maybe not, but I think that's exactly what it is."

"Well, if that's the case it's even more reason not to open it, or even touch it for that matter. Now, what about the bank?"

"Simmons said that there was a letter in his safety deposit box down at the bank that is supposed to tell all the people and what they did to that girl. He told the crowd enough to cause a stir. It was bad, Scott."

"If it happened." Scott pushed past Carl and headed down the embankment. "Everyone just move back. This is an active investigation site now. Anyone messing with that box gets arrested for tampering with evidence, I swear to God. Nobody touches it."

The crowd let out a disappointed moan as they parted to allow the sheriff passage. "I will need statements from everyone here. I suggest you all go home and put pen to paper and get it ready. You can come by the station tomorrow and sign them in front of witnesses."

The crowd slowly began to disperse, mumbling their discontent as they went.

Scott radioed for help and put a call into Barney Grimes, the town lawyer. His lazy Sunday afternoon was now shot to hell, and probably most of the night as well.

"You think there's a body in there?" he asked, looking at Carl Henson, who had followed him from his patrol car.

"If you heard what Simmons said you'd think it too. He pretty much came out and said it. We all heard it."

The sheriff sighed heavily. This could be the biggest thing that ever happened here and there was the possibility of trouble. He knew his three-man team couldn't handle something like this. Everyone called him sheriff, but in truth, he was just a small-town police chief and from the looks of things, he was either already in deeper shit than he could handle, or he soon would be.

He rubbed his eyes and shook his head, sparing the box another look. What sat before him looked like nothing more than a mud-caked, slimy wooden box, maybe an old shipping crate. He wanted to believe that was all it was, but he'd already heard enough to know it wasn't.

"Dammit," he growled. "I'm going to have to call in the county Sheriff, hell, maybe even the State police. I don't want this thing to go sideways."

"From what me and everyone else already heard sideways might not be so bad. If you ask me this thing is going to turn this whole town on its head."

"That's what I'm afraid of." Scott walked past his friend as the town's only other police car arrived. He waved the patrolmen down to where he stood.

"Curtiss, you stay here and make sure nobody, and I mean nobody, touches this box. Me and Bobby are going to run over to Rutherford Simmons' field and look around. I'll be back to relieve you in a bit. It looks like we're going to be in for a long night."

"What's in the box, Chief?"

"That is yet to be determined. You just make sure nobody touches it. Got that?"

"Yessir. I got it."

Carl Henson watched as the two officers climbed back up the muddy embankment and got into the patrol car. They tore off across the bridge headed to Rutherford Simmons' place.

The thing that surprised me the most was how quickly people took sides. Everyone in town was on one side or the other and that made for a contentious late spring and early summer. One side wanted the men prosecuted to the extent of the law, one wanted to drop the whole matter entirely, given the age and condition of the men in question.

One thing that I still find unsettling to this day is that some people, probably more than admitted it, wanted to see the body. I couldn't imagine anything that I'd want to see less than what was left of that poor girl.

Of course, another source of contention was the letter. People wanted to see that too. There were rumors that when the police opened that safety deposit box, that he'd found some jewelry and a very long letter detailing who was present and who did what during the "incident". That's what people were calling it. I suspect the fine Christian people of Pine Valley couldn't bring themselves to say the words "gangrape" and "murder", even with the caveat "alleged" in front of them.

The Sheriff closed the lid on the safe box and took it straight to his office and contacted the town lawyer, who also happened to be the only lawyer within fifty miles. Barney Grimes told the Sheriff to contact the state's attorney so that's what he did. The whole process was hush-hush, so new rumors surfaced almost every day.

Many of us younger folks tried to not get caught up in the whole mess, but it was impossible not to. The men alleged to have been involved touched so many of our lives. They were our grandfathers, summertime employers, and generally the backbone of the town. Every facet of our lives ran through at least one of the old men and now all of that was in limbo. The fact that most of the men didn't plow and plant, rebuild or clean up the property, or even paint fences left many of us boys without something to do after school let out.

The whole town seemed to have a black cloud hanging over it. In my own house, I saw my grandfather cry- although only briefly before my dad yelled at me to go outside. There were also a lot of hushed conversations, both with and about my grandfather. Several not-so-hushed arguments left a tense pall over the place, so I tried to stay away as much as possible.

It seemed that even my own house was on opposite sides of the fence about what happened, and my heart ached for both of my parents.

After spending half an hour working up the nerve, I asked my mother about it one day and she told me it wasn't none of my concern, but she looked at me with a strange look on her face. Like she wanted to tell me something but didn't want to either. She looked angry and sad at the same time.

I never asked dad.

A couple of weeks after the scene at the creekside a shiny black car appeared in town. It was a BMW and looked about as out of place in our little town as lipstick on a pig.

The car belonged to Arnold Fleischmann, lawyer for the defense. Many of the men met with him out at David Xavier's place to discuss the case. I don't know what was said or done, but that night Charles Green went home, put a shotgun in his mouth, and pulled the trigger.

His family found him in his barn, sitting on a hay bale with what was left of the back of his head splattered all over the weathered gray boards of a barn he'd inherited from his father. They had a closed casket and a private graveside service. I don't remember anyone in town going, which I thought was very odd. Maybe the family asked it that way, maybe his contemporaries figured they had enough blood on their hands and didn't want to add his to the mix.

As the weeks drug past, some people in town began compiling lists of who they thought was involved in the "incident". The persistent rumor was that there were a dozen boys present, and Rutherford Simmons already said that the former Sheriff's son was there. Everyone added both sons, Lester, and Lewis Anderson even though Lewis had died of cancer over five years before the box resurfaced. Of course, everyone had David Alexander, and when the news broke that Luscious Belau was found dead in his home, an empty bottle of his heart pills in his hand, everyone added him too.

Another name that most everyone had on their list was my grandfather, Robert McCloud. It pained me to no end, but deep down I knew his name belonged there. He and David Xavier were the main ones arguing against opening the box when we found it and, given his anxiety before and after, I knew he was guilty. It hurt my soul to think such things about the gentile old man who lived in our home, the man I'd known my whole life as "pawpaw".

I didn't want to believe it at first, but that all changed one Saturday morning when mom and dad were sleeping in and I was in the kitchen making myself some toast. Pawpaw walked into the kitchen looking like he hadn't slept well. When he saw me, he looked like he'd seen a ghost, or maybe a mirror. Standing in the doorway, his robe hanging loosely on his slumped shoulders, unshaven, with his hair in disarray, he looked defeated.

He took in a long, wheezy breath and shook his head. "I'm sorry," was all he said before turning and shuffling back to his room. That was all the confirmation I needed. It didn't matter how many motions the lawyer filed, how many statutes he cited, I knew my grandfather had done this terrible thing, and the heart that wanted so badly for him to be innocent broke.

The weight of what he'd done fell on my teenage shoulders like an anvil, pushing my spirit to the ground. I went out onto the back porch and sat on the steps and cried my eyes out. I cried for my family, my grandfather, Sophia, and Rutherford Simmons. I cried for the whole town and the other families hurt by the actions of a group of stupid, mean boys.

I spent most of that summer going between righteous indignation and outright sorrow. The disillusionment was hard on a lot of us, especially the boys. Our Grandfathers were active in our lives, teaching us, admonishing us when we did wrong, spoiling us from time to time. To us, they were old and wise, examples of how we should behave. They were our fathers' fathers. They were pioneers, founders of the town in which we lived. They were our *papaws* for goodness sake.

They were also rapists. Every time I forced myself to admit that it was like swallowing a cocklebur.

The day that the summons went out, everyone watched closely. The county clerk drove back and forth across town, escorted by the Sheriff, and stopped at the houses in question.

A bunch of us guys was hanging out in front of the hardware store drinking Cokes because it had a long awning that provided us some shade. We watched it stop at the Anderson house at one end of Chester Street, then at the Dunn's place on the other.

The scene reminded me of that movie "The Ten Commandments." In the movie, the curse traveled throughout the city, embodied by an ominous green smoke that slithered along the ground, stopping at some houses while passing others by. In each house visited there were shrieks of terror, of pleading that it was a mistake. But it wasn't a mistake. The plague of death came to the houses it was intended to visit, and so did the county clerk.

David Xavier, Lester Anderson, Paul Cummings, Matthew Dunn, Andrew Foley, Mortimer Klein, Adolphus Landon, and Robert McCloud were all charged in the incident that day. Lewis Anderson, Luscious Belau, Johnny Helms, and Charles Green were also implicated, posthumously. That raised the ire of many folks and was seen as "speaking ill of the dead", but the DA said it was important, in case anyone wanted to file a civil suit against their estates.

The town erupted that night, some celebrated their exoneration, and some withdrew in the light of the confirmation of what many people had already pieced together. When word got out about the ones charged, I suspect that more than one household kept a shotgun at the ready in case of trouble. Fortunately, there was only a lot of name-calling and two acts of vandalism, but not much else. Someone threw red paint on Matthew Dunn's front door and Lewis Anderson's tombstone was shattered with a sledgehammer. The Sheriff attributed this as much to personal problems someone might have had with the families as much as the charges. There were other issues in the past that didn't make it to the supper table conversation either.

It was the worst summer of my life. My whole world was turned upside down and I resented the men who had done it. The innocence we'd all enjoyed growing up in a small, rural town was in shambles around our feet and we didn't know how to go on. The granddaughters of the men implicated at least had each other's shoulders to cry on. We guys tried to tough it out, downplaying, or outright ignoring what was happening. For me, at least, that approach wasn't working. I was anxious to do something, anything, that would make it right. Sadly, there was no making this right. It had happened and there was nothing ever going to make it right.

Thankfully, the trial was moved to the county seat and our little town was spared the spectacle of watching our founding fathers be grilled by the District Attorney. A lot of people made the forty-seven-mile trip to watch the trial. Some made it every day, but I didn't. I only went once. The look on my own Grandfather's face was enough for me. He was guilty and that was bad enough.

Still, details filtered their way back to our tiny hamlet that, up to now, was about as boring as they come. I overheard Fran Young telling Susan Anderson (no relation to Lester and Lewis) about how David Xavier went first with the girl and how he kept going back, even to the point that he and Andrew Foley fought over whose turn it was. When the two women saw me standing within earshot, waiting to pay for the lunch my mom and I had just eaten, they both blushed and Susan slipped away quickly. She told Fran she'd call her later.

Another day I heard a conversation about how violent Luscious Belau was, slapping the girl repeatedly while he was having her. When they mentioned his laugh, my blood ran cold, and I decided I had somewhere else to be.

Luscious was a nice man who always had a good joke, especially for the teenage boys he ran across. Every time he told one, he would throw his head back and let loose a full, throaty laugh so genuine you'd think he'd heard the joke for the first time. His laugh was always a pleasant memory to me, until that day. After that, I couldn't imagine anything else but him slapping that poor girl over and over.

Every day during the trial, my father would put on the only suit he owned, help his father put on the only suit he owned, and they would drive to the trial. My grandfather, Paul Cummings, and Andrew Foley were the only three that came back to town. The rest of the accused opted to stay away from Pine Valley, which might have been best.

Every night we had supper in silence. Sometimes my grandfather would join us, sometimes not. On the nights that he did, I would steal glances at him, wondering what evils he'd perpetrated on the girl and on Rutherford Simmons. Had he hit her too? Did he beat Mr. Simmons? Even if he didn't, he was there, and he participated. He also left two people for dead and spent the rest of his life lying about it. I didn't want to hate him, but a lifetime of adoration felt so far away.

The kindly hands that helped teach me to tie my shoes became weapons. His understanding smile became a lustful, sinister grin. I couldn't help thinking that all of it had been a lie.

He was a rapist and a murderer.

I also stole glimpses at my father. He was being a dutiful son, transporting the man who had raised him back and forth four days a week. He was sitting through the gory details and the arguments every day, and my respect for him grew tenfold. His eyes were angry despite his attempts to hide it. He had always been a rule follower, a by-the-book kind of guy and I knew this was killing him. He already looked ten years older.

One night my dad was talking to my mother on the porch. The hushed tones got my attention, and I knew better than to eavesdrop, but I couldn't help myself. Perhaps it was youthful curiosity or some morbid desire to know who did what, but I snuck around the house and crept up in the dark behind my mother's azalea bushes and laid on the dry ground listening.

"That damned Jew lawyer is trying to get everyone to say they can't remember nothing. He calls it 'circumstantial' evidence and is making out in court that Mr. Simmons is a crazy old man that makes up stories. He spent all day objecting to everything the DA said and talking about how Mr. Simmons never married because he was a queer and that he's a weirdo."

"I know it's hard, dear. Why don't you just drop him off and spend the day at the park or something? There's no need to listen to all the details."

"I don't know." He sighed heavily. "I just wish I didn't have to go in the first place."

"I know, sweetie. I know it's hard to sit there all day and listen to this stuff about your father."

"That's just it. They're not even calling no names. It's all 'defendant one, defendant two'. Stuff like that. You'd need a chart to even know who did what. It just doesn't make sense. Dad said the first thing the lawyer told them was not to say anything to nobody, not even him. Don't admit anything. Can you believe that?"

"Times are changing. Lawyers want to win, that's why I don't trust 'em."

"It all feels like some twisted game. I don't know how much more I can stand. It's ruining our whole family."

"Well, whether he's found guilty or not, I think things have changed. The whole town has changed."

"Do you think it's changed? The same people doing the same thing. Now the truth is just out in the open instead of being exchanged in glances and certain looks. Those men all know what happened and every time they see each other they have to admit it to one another. Even though they might never have spoken of it again. They know that everyone else there knows."

"But is that punishment enough? That's what they're trying to decide up at the courthouse."

"Tomorrow they're going to read the letter Rutherford Simmons wrote back then after it happened. I don't even know if I wanna hear it or not. Probably not."

"I wouldn't."

"I've already heard too much. All dad does is cry all the way there and back and say he doesn't want to talk about it. It just doesn't seem real."

"No, it doesn't. But it is, and so are the effects. Something happened and they're just now sorting out the who and what."

"Does that make much of a difference at this point? I mean, is any one of them more or less guilty than the others?"

"Honey, I don't want to tell you what to do, but I'd drop your dad off and wait for him. You don't need to hear the details."

I heard my father's heavy sigh. "You're probably right. It's just that the wondering is almost as bad as the knowing. Know what I mean?"

"I know. It's six of one or half dozen of another and all the eggs are rotten."

The silver-haired judge banged his gavel hard and looked around the packed courtroom, his face casting a stern warning to the crowd.

"The bailiff will now read into evidence the letter written by Rutherford Barns Simmons, as written, including all relevant names and places. He will read it verbatim with no regard to grammar and punctuation. I have considered the defense's objections and do think the evidence needs to be read as written.

"I caution all of you to maintain your decorum and remember that this is a court of law. I also want you to remember that this trial does need to have a gallery to continue. The outbursts over the last few days will not be tolerated any further. If you interrupt these proceedings, you will be removed from my courtroom."

His eyes swept the crowd from left to right, driving home his warning as the bailiff, a short, stocky man with his hair well-oiled and swept to one side, stepped nervously to the microphone situated in front of the judge's bench. In his hand, he clutched several loose sheets of paper that were older than he was. He cleared his throat and raised the papers before him.

"Sophia Magladoni was the most beautiful girl in the world and I'm not even going to lie and say I wasn't head over heels in love with her. She had long, dark hair and green eyes that sparkled like the sun, and a laugh that could make a man's soul catch fire. She was- "

"Stop right there."

I looked down from my perch in the gallery, hidden from my daddy by two hulking bodies of men I didn't know, at the man who had spoken up. Unlike most of the people in the courtroom, I recognized the voice. It was my grandfather.

The judge banged his gavel and called the court to order as a murmur rippled through the hot, stuffy air. "I said order!" he demanded.

"I ain't being out of order." Robert McCloud stood up from the defendant's table as the hands of his co-defendants tried to pull him back to his seat. He shrugged them off and looked at the judge.

"I don't wanna sit here and hear that letter. I don't wanna hear about what happened. I know what happened and I wanna change my plea to guilty."

The judge banged his gavel again harder. "Order. Everybody shut the hell up." He slid forward in his seat and leaned on his podium, looking down at the old man standing before him. "You might want to confer with your attorney, sir."

"I don't need to do nothing of the sort." Arnold Fleischmann stood and said something to him, but he pushed him away. "I ain't gonna say nothing but admit to what I did. I owe it to my family to keep 'em from having to go through all this. What I did is killing my boy and his family and they don't deserve this."

"Are you saying that you want to separate yourself from the group and pursue a different avenue of legal action?" the judge asked.

"If that means that I wanna change my pleading from innocent to guilty, then yessir, that's exactly what I'm a saying."

The judge banged his gavel several times and threatened to clear the courtroom as the murmur grew into a low rumble. "At this time I declare a recess so that this defendant can have an opportunity to seek legal counsel and decide upon his course of action. However, seeing that you have confessed to the crimes leveled against you, the bailiff will remove this defendant to my quarters. I will personally advise the defendant of his rights at that time." He slammed the gavel down hard once and declared the trial in recess for one hour.

The crowd below erupted in movement as a cacophony of voices swept up to the gallery, but my eyes were on my father. He was sitting in the third row on the right side of the courtroom. As the people around him thinned, I saw him lean forward, prop his elbows on his knees and cover his face with his hands. I couldn't tell if he was relieved or upset. The way he sat there, still as a knot on a log, I figured he was both in equal parts.

The remaining defendants and their lawyer watched the bailiff remove my grandfather, then turned to look at my father. In their eyes, I saw anger and betrayal, but to me, it looked like hypocrisy. They all knew the men were at least as guilty as Robert McCloud but didn't have the guts to own up to it. They all looked like cowards to me.

I caught a ride back to town in the back of a Chevy pick-up. The driver, a middle-aged man that I vaguely recognized, offered me a seat in the cab, but I declined. He'd surely want to talk about the trial and that was the last thing I wanted to do. My mind and my heart were experiencing a tornado of emotions and I needed time to sort them out. I sat in the back of the truck and cried while the wind tore at my hair. I didn't know what I was crying for exactly, but I cried just the same.

When my father came home without his father, he and mom went into the bedroom and talked for a long time. I tried to look like I was interested in the television show when they came out and sat on the couch together.

"We need to tell you something, son."

"Okay." I switched off the set and looked at the two faces that I had seen every day of my life, but they looked different than they had ever looked before. My mother looked sad, with a little aggravation and maybe a little bit of indignation. My father looked beleaguered, defeated, and sad.

But there was also a little bit of relief in his eyes. At least it was over.

"They kept your pawpaw in jail," my father started, rubbing his big hands together. The palms, rough from years of construction work sounded like two pieces of sandpaper. "He confessed to…." his voice trailed off as his gaze fell to his hands. He looked up at me and said, "Everything."

I nodded, trying not to let on that I knew. "Maybe that's for the best."

My father looked at me, his brow furrowed slightly as his tired eyes searched my face, trying to figure me out. "I guess it is, in the end."

"Maybe now, we can begin to put this whole thing behind us and move on as a family." My dad didn't look at my mom when she spoke, absorbing the sting of her comments without a flinch.

I did cast a wide-eyed look her way, for which I received a stern stare that I was only able to hold for a few seconds. When an eyebrow arched slightly, I broke and dropped my gaze to my hands. When I looked up, they were gone, and I was glad to be alone.

Although my father was spared the details of the letter in court, enough filtered its way back home to piece the puzzle together. The letter turned out to be a longer version of what Rutherford Simmons told us that day by the creek, with names and details that kept the gossip mill busy for weeks around town. Everywhere you went people were talking about it.

The knot that had been in my stomach before my grandfather confessed grew and spread to my chest. I hated the fact that everyone was enjoying the gossip a little too much. Families talked about what others did but brushed over what their own patriarch had done as if merely raping her was better than hitting her while you raped her. The typical small-town hypocrisy was in high spirits and I hated every minute of it.

As summer staggered in and the heat began to mount, I found myself growing more and more aggravated with the people I'd known my whole life. The whole town took on an anxious persona as they awaited the verdict. The trial lingered into June, with the attorney for the defense throwing everything in the book at the DA to win the case, but as the temperatures began to rise the judge's lenience grew shorter and he ordered closing statements.

They say Arnold Fleischmann strutted and crowed for three hours as he surmised the impossibility of a guilty verdict. The DA had Rutherford Simmons' letter Xeroxed and gave each juror a copy. "If you can't find the truth in these pages", he was rumored to have said, "then you can't find it anywhere." That was all he said. He stood and looked into the eyes of the jury and shook his head sadly before walking back to his table.

I sat across the street from Barney Grimes' office for an hour, looking at the faded sign hanging against the red brick building. The words 'One nation, under God, with liberty and justice for all' had once been bright red against the black shingle of wood but had faded considerably after so many southern summers. It seemed a perfect indictment of what was happening in our town. Justice had faded into a distant memory, but it wasn't forgotten entirely.

I knew that just inside that weathered gray door next to the sign, the town lawyer was sitting at his desk and that he was probably going over somebody's will. He mostly did minor legal work and had nothing to do with the case that took over the town, but he was handling Rutherford Simmons' affairs and that was why I wanted to see him.

When I finally got up the nerve to walk inside, he greeted me with a smile and a cold drink.

"I was wondering if you were going to come in today."

I nodded sheepishly but said nothing. This wasn't the first day I'd stood outside his office.

"You got anything wrong? Or is this a social call?" he asked in his usual pleasant demeanor.

"No. I mean, nothing's wrong. I ain't in any trouble or nothing."

"I didn't think so," he said with a smile as he leaned back in his chair. "So why don't you tell me what's brought you down here?"

I shook my head and sipped my coke as I tried to gather my jumble of thoughts into a coherent sentence. "It's just wrong, you know." I shook my head again. "I mean, they got the trial and everything. All that business. But ain't nobody even thought about the girl. Not about her, her family, or anything. Everybody's talking about what happened to her, what they might or might not have done to her. Hell, I think some folks even enjoy talking about the dirty stuff in some kind of perverted game or something. What the holy hell is wrong with people? I mean-"

The look of surprise on Barney Grimes' face made me realize that my voice was steadily rising and by the time I caught myself I was nearly shouting.

"I'm sorry." I took another sip of the coke and sank into the cracked leather of the chair. "It's just, I mean, I can't stop thinking about this poor girl and her family. They must have wondered what happened to her, where she was. Don't you think?"

Barney nodded and sighed. "I don't see how they couldn't. They were a traveling show. Probably drifters, maybe gypsies. I don't know. Back then things were different. They left town and never raised a stink about it. One can only assume that they either knew the answer they'd get if they did, or maybe they were too afraid to say anything in the first place."

"But how could they just leave without her?"

"I don't know, son. It's hard to imagine now, but things were a lot different back then. Especially in a small town like this. They say this was a rough place back in the hay days."

"But did anyone ever think to look for them?"

"And tell them what? That their daughter was…. well, you know. Maybe it was better to just let them hope she ran off and got married or something."

"It still doesn't seem right."

"It doesn't. And in the great tragedy of things a young woman lost her life and a young man's life was irrevocably changed. Did you happen to notice that when the events took place, the boys in question were all around your age? Now they're practically dead with old age."

I nodded in agreement as I pondered the comparison, telling myself that me and a group of my friends weren't capable of such a thing, that something like that couldn't happen anymore. Somewhere deep down inside I knew I was wrong, but I let myself believe it anyway. I needed to believe it then and I still do now.

"As a man of the court, I want to believe that justice finds its man, even if it takes time, but I don't know if justice can ever be reaped from the thing that was sown that day so long ago. Too much time has passed." Barney Grimes looked out his window as an old pickup rattled past.

"So that's it? We just chalk it up as a tragedy and move on?" I didn't want to accept the cold truth. "There has to be something to exact justice somehow."

"And what do you suggest? Lock up some old men? Should we beat them? Hang them? Would that alleviate the years of turmoil this family endured? Does inflicting pain and agony on the family of those guilty even the score? Their own families, hell, this whole town has been victimized. How do we exact justice for that?"

I nodded again as my chest swelled with agony. It felt like my whole life was a lie. My kindly old pawpaw was a rapist and a murderer. The admission shook me to my core and sent a shudder through my spine.

"Sometimes the system fails us, but it's the only system we got. People like that judge and the DA try to do what they can do to get justice, to punish the guilty. But, unfortunately, sometimes it just misses the chance to do it in a timely manner."

"You're a lawyer, do you think they will be found guilty?"

Barney shrugged and ran a hand over his hair as he stared out the window. When he looked back at me, his face was painted with genuine sadness. He shook his head.

"That's bullshit."

"That it is, my young friend. That it is."

"The DA and I talk a lot. Professional courtesy, I guess. Your pawpaw didn't implicate anyone in his confession. It's just Rutherford Simmons' letter against seven men who suddenly can't remember anything."

"So my pawpaw stands up and does the right thing and he may be the only one punished?"

"Unfortunately so."

The injustice of the situation hit me like a ton of bricks. How, in a so-called civilized world could this happen? How could any of this happen?

"I know it stinks, but I do have some other news." Barney went to a filing cabinet and retrieved an old cigar box. Sitting it on his desk, he opened it to reveal a necklace lying atop a nest of cotton balls. "Mr. Simmons left a detailed will. In it, he agreed to pay my hourly rate for every minute I spent looking for the family of Sophia Magladoni. He wanted the necklace returned. It was a family thing, a rite of passage for the girls. He wasn't very clear on that, but he was clear on the fact of having it returned to the family. He did mention a sister, but not a name."

I slid forward, staring at the necklace. A small blue stone no bigger than a good-sized kernel of corn sat atop the old cotton balls. A thin gold chain snaked its way through the yellowing clumps of cotton. It wasn't anything fancy, but its lure hooked me the instant I saw it.

In the weeks after I first saw it, I imagined it new and shiny, sparkling in the sun as it lay against the skin of a young, beautiful Sophia Magladoni. I imagined her hand going to it unconsciously as she went about her day, making sure it was still there. A simple gift that meant the world to a girl who probably had so little.

Even when the verdict came in not guilty and the whole town erupted, choosing sides all over again, I concentrated on the small sapphire and kept the image in the forefront of my mind. The jury's decision saddened me, but it didn't surprise me. Barney had warned me against hoping for a guilty verdict. Even if they're found guilty, he said one day, they will probably never spend a day in jail. Their age and their health, which would quickly deteriorate if they were found guilty, would keep that from happening.

Some of the men returned to town. Some didn't. Andrew Foley's family sent him to a nursing home a few counties over, and Adolphus London went to a hospital. He lasted a few weeks but died of congestive heart failure. The other five men mostly stayed home and out of the public eye, allowing their families to absorb the looks of ridicule and shame in their stead.

After the verdict, a lot of people moved on from the excitement of the "incident". The heat was almost unbearable that summer and a neighboring county opened a water park. Within a few months of the decision, people just stopped talking about it, a fact that I found incredibly odd.

That whole summer and into the fall I spent a lot of time in Barney Grimes' office. He taught me how to use his computer and how to search databases. As a lawyer, he gained access to information and names that would have been impossible for me to access.

We compiled a list of possible relatives, focusing on potential sisters, and one Wednesday I called over thirty people across the whole southern United States. Some of them listened to my story and congratulated me on my efforts even though they weren't related to the Magladoni family. Some said they didn't know them and hung up quickly. One man said he knew the family, then asked me to meet him at the welcome center on interstate 10 just inside the Louisiana line. He told me to come alone and sounded a little too eager, so I hung up.

The next day I called another twenty names and got the same result, except for the pervert in Louisiana. When I crossed the last name off the list, I looked at Barney and threw my hands up.

"Giving up?"

"What else can we do?" I asked.

"We can take a break. Let it simmer. Sometimes when you stir the pot something comes to the top. Don't lose heart. Go home and don't think about it for a few days. You've been spending a lot of time in this office. Go hang out with your friends, maybe take a girl out on a date or something. Do anything to take your mind off this."

I sighed, knowing he was right. I had been calling myself a "legal assistant" all summer and accepting a meager pittance from Mr. Simmons' estate for my efforts, but my absence from my group of friends was becoming conspicuous. My mother's patience was also growing thin with my "unhealthy obsession". I left the office with the promise to return at nine a.m. sharp Monday morning, but Barney said to make it ten-thirty.

By the time summer faded into fall things were returning to normal. People rarely brought up the "incident" unless one of the men happened to appear in town. The long, hot summer full of intrigue, suspicion, and gossip turned into an optimistic fall as the riot of colorful leaves began to appear in Pine Valley. The leads that Barney and I had to chase down had slowed to a trickle and I spent a lot of time just hanging out and daydreaming while he did his usual legal work.

I spent Halloween night hanging out with my friends, drinking beer, and flirting with Sandra Holcomb, a red-haired beauty that I had admired from afar all through our senior year. She had a good, sturdy build and a smattering of freckles across the bridge of her nose. As we sat on the tailgate of the beat-up Ford that my father handed down to me, the smell of her perfume and the warmth of her body next to me all but erased any memory of Sophia Magladoni and her necklace.

The next few weeks were a pleasant respite from the tedious work I'd thrown myself into and, as much as I hate to admit it, the desire to be with Sandra was surpassing the need to return the necklace. That is until the call came in that changed everything.

I was greeted by a loud honking as Barney blew his nose when I walked into his office. He warned me to stay back and said he thought he had the flu, then played the message left on his answering machine. The voice on the machine was that of a man who sounded to be about the same age as my father. He said that his mother's maiden name was Magladoni, but if they were looking for money, they were barking up the wrong tree.

"He left a number and I called him back. It took some doing, but I finally convinced him we weren't debtors." Andy sneezed into a tissue and blew his nose again. "He told me his mother was very old and in poor health. She's in a nursing home in Missouri. He gave me the name. I called and got the address."

I looked at the scrap of paper that Barney held up before him like it was the Holy Grail. It was the best chance we had, and possibly one of the last. "What should we do?"

"I, my young friend, am going to the doctor, then I am going home. I feel awful."

"So that's it? We do nothing?"

Barney sneezed again. "For me, for a week or so, yes. But, knowing that you are young and impatient, I am willing to commission you to deliver the package."

"But how do we know it's the right person?"

"I talked to the guy for a long time. It's the right one. He said his mother was in a traveling circus when she was a kid until she met a man in Missouri and married him. He said she always talked about a sister that he never met. Her maiden name was Ethelinda Magladoni.

I broke a date with Sandra and drove the 517 miles to Des Arc, Missouri. It was a small town, smaller even than Pine Valley, so finding the nursing home wasn't difficult. When I pulled up, I was floored by the name of the place. Pine Valley Skilled Nursing Facility. I sat in my old truck for more than a few minutes wondering about the forces of nature at work. Was it Divine intervention, or one of those odd coincidences that lead me from Pine Valley, Alabama to the Pine Valley Skilled Nursing Facility in Des Arc, Missouri? Whatever force brought me to this place demanded that I see things through and return to its rightful owner a necklace that had laid in a safety deposit box for almost seventy years.

After I lied and told her I was a grandson, a nurse at the front desk pointed me to room one eleven. I walked down the hall, becoming aware of the faint smell of urine and sense of desperation that seemed to emanate from the pale, yellow walls that surrounded me. It was a sad place and it made me sad to be there.

I knocked gently on door eleven and pushed it open cautiously. The bed closest to the door was empty, but the frail form of a woman occupied the bed next to the window. Alerted by the knock and the squeak of the door as it opened, the old woman's head rolled toward me, her eyes finding mine instantly.

I froze for a moment, staring at her. Although old and wrinkled, she looked like the sort of woman who was once beautiful, and I wondered if she looked like her sister. If she did there was little wonder Rutherford Simmons fell in love so easily.

"Hi," I began nervously. "You don't know me but- "

"Come and sit awhile." Her voice was coarse and sounded tired despite the smile that slipped across her thin lips.

"Yes, ma'am." I took up a seat next to the bed, the cigar box clutched in my hands resting on my lap. "You don't know me, but I know your sister."

The smile faded from the old woman's lips as her eyes searched my face, her brow furrowing slightly.

"Sophia?" she asked quietly as if she hadn't spoken the name in many years.

"Yes."

The smile returned to her lips. "I haven't seen her in a lifetime. Is she here?"

"No ma'am. I'm sorry."

"That's okay, I didn't think she was. I was just hoping." She took in a long, ragged breath and exhaled slowly. "Has she passed on?"

"Unfortunately so. I hate to be the bearer of bad news but-"

"I was ten years old last time I saw her. We used to travel around in this travelin' show, you know."

"Yes ma'am. I know."

"I always thought it was exciting. Traveling by train. Visiting so many different places. Meeting new people every few weeks."

"I'm from Pine Valley, Alabama, ma'am."

The woman's eyes narrowed as she stared at me. She swallowed hard and began to speak, "Pine Valley? That was the name of the town where my sister, Sophia, ran away. We never saw her again. I cried and cried when we left that town without her. My papa said she'd run off and met a man, most likely since she was close to marrying age and all. Said she never liked the travelin' life much." She paused to catch her breath as she shook her head. "I loved my sister so much. She was so beautiful. Everyone said so. I remember lying in bed with her every night and talking about everything. Life, travelin', men. She was six years older than me. We had a brother born between us, but he died of the polio."

"I'm sorry to hear that."

A sad smile came to her face and she sighed. "It was sad. A lot of things were sad for us back then."

"I'm sorry for that too."

"It's okay. Things are different now. Things are better."

"Ma'am, the reason I'm here is to return something to you." I lifted the cigar box and opened it.

Her eyes widened and her mouth fell open when she saw the necklace. She drew in a deep breath and put a hand to her wrinkled throat.

"We thought you should have this."

Her hands shook as she reached inside the loose gown covering her chest and produced a similar necklace. Hers carried a gem the same size and shape as the one in the box, but the stone was red. She raised it and kissed the stone with her thin lips.

"You did know my Sophia. It's a miracle."

"Well, I wouldn't say that-"

"Are you her child, or I guess grandchild?"

I sighed heavily, absorbing the old woman's hopeful gaze. "In a way, I guess you could say we're kin."

She clasped her hands together and smiled. "I was so afraid for her. You see, we are gypsies. I don't know if she ever told you that. But we traveled around and did shows and entertained people, but they didn't like us too much. When I was a young girl, I never understood why. We were just people, different perhaps, but just people, nonetheless. My mother was so scared when Sophia didn't come back that night. She said that she knew in her heart something bad had happened. My father searched everywhere but never found any sign of her. He told mama she must have run off with some fella, you know. He said a local boy was hanging around who'd taken a shine to Sophia. But mama was so sad for so long. She cried and cried. Every night. Papa said she ran off and so we left. I never heard from her again. Not even the first letter." The old woman wiped a tear from her cheek with a boney finger. "I always hoped she'd run off and gotten married."

"Things are complicated."

"Oh, I never blamed her. Papa said she ran off and married and forgot all her old ways. When I'd ask about her, he'd say I bet she's got this big old farmhouse and a good husband and lots of kids and chickens." She smiled. He told me that every time, so I guess I believed him. Life wasn't easy. It was a lot of hard work."

"Yes, ma'am. I guess it was."

"I guess if you're here, she must have told you about her old life, and about us."

"Of sorts," I lied, not wanting to upset the old woman.

"So tell me about her. Is she your grandmother?"

I opened my mouth to tell her about Sophia and about what happened to her. I intended to tell her about the boys who had raped her, the men they grew into, and the trial, about my grandfather and what they did to her sister. I intended to come clean to exact some manner of justice, but I didn't.

I closed my mouth without saying a word and stared into the tired, anxious eyes of the old woman I'd just met a few minutes ago and realized what a fool's errand I'd been on.

What was justice if it robbed an old woman of a pleasant memory? What was truth if it inflicted needless pain on a woman who had already suffered a lifetime of missing her sister? What end would it serve to send her to her grave with hate and bitterness in her heart?

In the end, I sighed and forced a smile. When I opened my mouth, I lied to the old woman. I told her about how Sophia Magladoni was the jewel of Pine Valley, that she was the most beautiful woman anyone had ever seen. I talked about her elegance and her humility. I invented memories of a woman well-loved and admired, of a woman who married a man who wasn't rich, except in honor and appreciation for his

125

beautiful bride. I told her how she was cherished by all of her children and revered by her grandchildren. I spoke of a woman fiercely loyal to her family and her beliefs, a strong woman with a tender heart. I told her of a man who never loved anyone else as much as he loved her sister.

I wiped a tear from my eye when I told of her funeral. And how she was laid to rest on a hill, far from the reach of floodwaters where the sunshine was plentiful and the wildflowers abundant. I spoke of how the man that loved her until his last breath was laid to rest beside her.

Somewhere along the way, I realized that I was telling the story of how I thought her life might have been with Rutherford Simmons if that day next to Bitterweed Creek had never happened. I told the story that I wished had happened instead of the truth about the one that did.

When I finished talking, we were both crying and exchanged a long embrace. I took the necklace out of the cigar box and placed it around her neck. She lifted the stones and kissed them both.

"I cannot thank you enough, young man."

"It was my pleasure, ma'am."

"I have to admit something. I lied before." She cleared her throat and asked for a glass of water. "My daddy always said that about Sophia, but I never believed him. I believed mama that something bad happened to her. She wasn't the first girl to come up missing. I even had a few things happen to me along the way. So, you see, I was sure that something bad had to have happened to her." She let out a tired sigh.

"All these years I believed it. It was always a great source of pain for my mother, and for me too. I'm old, in case you haven't noticed, and I don't have many days left here on this earth. It's been an unspoken source of pain for me to not know what happened to her. You've given an old woman peace in her last days and I can't thank you enough."

"I'm glad I could do it. Really." I smiled at her and tried to excuse myself, but she asked me to stay a while longer. I answered all her questions with beautiful, elaborate lies about a life that was never lived. I told her amusing anecdotes that never happened and laughed when she laughed.

By the time the shadows were growing long, and they brought her supper tray, I was emotionally drained, but genuinely happy. The old woman's eyes beamed with life and her laughter had long since chased away the pall of sadness that hung over the room when I first arrived.

I hugged her again before I left, wrapping her in a strong embrace that lasted a long time. She clasped her hands together around both necklaces and thanked me for all that I had done, but the joy and relief in her eyes told me all I needed to hear.

What started as a quest for some kind of reparation for an unknown evil brought upon her family ended as a bestowing of peace upon a lonely old woman coasting toward the end of her life.

As I drove home in the dark, with only the sounds of the road and an old truck to keep me company, I wondered if it was a more worthy purpose in life to be a harbinger of peace and calm to those who need it most or to cast the cloak of innocence or guilt upon those whose evil may be well hidden within their hearts. I didn't know what atrocities this woman might have wrought, just like I never could have predicted what the men in my hometown had done in their youth. Who is worthy of peace, and justice? Who deserved punishment? Freedom?

I never came up with a clear answer that night, nor since. I did realize, however, that certain words were more than simple words. Peace and justice were concepts, ideas that were multi-faceted and incredibly complex, and far beyond my small-town way of thinking.

I did resolve to never do anything, to hide in any box, any dark secret that may surface at some point down the road, leaving my kids and grandkids with a box to fish out of the river. It was the best I could do, and in the end, it might be the best legacy I could leave them.

Finding Caroline

Standing in the doorway of the dilapidated house in a pair of relaxed-fit Levi's and a plain blue T-shirt, Ben felt like a man on Mars. He didn't belong here. No one belonged in a place like this. The stench slowly began to build in his nostrils as he waited for his eyes to adjust from the bright sunshine outside to the dim light of the house. The chorus of smells assaulted his nose: sweat, urine, feces, sex, dust, mildew, and pain, all combined to produce one unforgettable scent. It was a smell of desperation, of rock bottom.

It wasn't the first time he'd encountered that particular smell in the last few years. Sometimes it was worse, sometimes less so, but it was heartbreaking every time. It all depended on how long the occupants had been using the house. That's exactly what they did. They used the house; they didn't live there. What they did there could scarcely be called living at all.

Taking a tentative step forward, Ben scanned the room. It used to be someone's living room at some point in its life, but now it was a dump. Various takeout containers occupied the far-right corner of the room. Mostly burger wrappers and pizza boxes scattered among a dozen or so empty beer cans. At least they've taken time to eat, he thought. That was something.

To his left, a dirty blanket lay wadded against the wall like the shed skin of a giant, filthy snake. A few spent needles littered the threadbare carpet next to it, along with a used condom. Ben's stomach tightened, but he didn't retch. He'd done his share of retching, but all that was behind him now. His hand subconsciously went to the .38 tucked into his belt beneath his clean shirt. This wasn't his first time inside a flophouse.

Running a hand through his thinning hair, he pulled his eyes away from the needles, not wanting to see them anymore. It was already warm in the house, but the sweat on his brow was from his distress. This was the second such place he'd searched today. In the first, he'd encountered a couple of junkies still coherent enough to give him some trouble. He considered putting a bullet in their head to end their miserable lives but settled for just pushing them back to the floor from which they rose. It didn't take much to subdue a junkie after they'd been strung out all night. Mostly they were sick and just wanted to sleep. There was no need to hurt them any more than they were hurting themselves. After all, they were someone's child too.

To his right, in what probably used to be a dining room, a ragged cloth hung over the window cast the room in an eerie glow. He looked at his arms as he entered the room, now covered in a yellow hue, and a word crawled into his mind. Sick.

A grimy queen-sized mattress lay in the corner, stained from one end to the other with what had to be a mixture of every fluid a body could produce. A dark blanket lay haphazardly across it, partially hiding a cast-off glass tube, the end that he could see was charred black. There were a few old condoms tossed into the corner at the foot of the mattress and an empty quart bottle of Southern Comfort Bourbon. You could get a lot of things from laying on the mattress, he thought, but comfort wasn't one of them, southern or otherwise.

Turning, he found a small fireplace surrounded by a mantelpiece that must have been beautiful at some point in its life. The white paint was now dingy, stained by years of neglect and dirty hands. Both pieces of the vertical ornate trim had been pulled off and burned in its own firebox. One last degradation to be suffered by the fine craftsmanship that was once a centerpiece of a family home. The mantel that probably held Christmas stockings and family treasures now supported an accumulation of empty beer bottles, cigarette butts, and a half-eaten cheeseburger.

Beside the fireplace a door, propped open with a brick, led to the kitchen. Ben slipped quietly into the room, his eyes looking for signs of life. In all the times he'd picked his way through houses just like this one, he'd had surprisingly little trouble. If anyone were around, they usually just threw stoned looks his way, their stares coming from a faraway world that he couldn't begin to imagine. Sometimes he saw shame, sometimes contempt, but usually the glances were empty and hopeless.

Turning to leave the kitchen, Ben caught sight of a rat as it scurried around the door and disappeared into the room he'd just left, headed straight for the mattress. He shook his head at the sight of the rat and took in a deep, worried breath. There were always rats. Always. And they always looked the same: scrawny, mean, and hungry.

Moving quickly, the thick soles of his boots thudding on the wooden floor, he passed back through the dining room and living room, finding a hallway that undoubtedly led to bedrooms.

He felt for his gun again as he carefully navigated the narrow passage where several rusty nails stuck out from the dusty walls, menacing him as he passed. Pausing, he noticed a few stray fibers that might have been hair clinging to one of them. What once held family memories now stood as booby traps, waiting to snare anyone who passed too close. Blowing gently, he watched the fibers dance in his breath, inspecting them carefully. Relieved, he could tell that they were some type of synthetic thread. Maybe polyester or rayon. More specifically it wasn't sandy brown hair. That was good, but it didn't mean a lot.

Moving on, he paused at the first door he came to. The battered, chipped paint said that it had been through hell, but then again, who hadn't. The old knob turned in his hand and the door swung open slightly, giving him a glimpse into the darkened room. Someone had blacked out the windows with something, most likely spray paint.

He retrieved a penlight from his left pants pocket and looked around the room. There was a bed in the corner and atop it, three naked bodies lay in a tangled heap. Putting the various limbs with their owner, he counted one black man, one black woman, and one white woman. Light fell on the man's face, glistening off the beads of sweat on his forehead. The girl in the middle laid mostly on her stomach with her bare ass on unapologetic display for anyone who cared to look. Ben moved the light quickly off her nakedness and found the other woman. As the light lingered on the white girl's face she stirred, mumbled something incoherent, and rolled over away from the beam, revealing a spine and rib cage that protruded angrily from her thin skin.

Taking a step back, he pulled the door closed and took a deep breath to clear his lungs of the hot, sweaty air that hung heavy in the room. It was the smell of humanity at its worst, of human beings robbed of dignity by whichever monster they choose to feed. It was the kind of smell that Ben could never have imagined from his comfortable suburban home; from the

133

relatively lofty heights of his middle-class life; from the mundane blue-collar existence he'd once had.

Of course, all that was a lifetime ago, before he'd been drug down from his perch into this nightmare. It was a life before his daughter, Caroline, met T.J.

Moving to the next door, he opened it slowly. There was no shade over the window, allowing the morning sun to illuminate the ugly scene before him. A fly buzzed past his head, eager to escape the stench. His stomach knotted instantly as he recoiled from the room, a wave of warm, putrid air washing over him. Pulling a washcloth, heavily sprinkled with his daughter's perfume, out of his back pocket he held it over his nose and mouth. The sweet, flowery smell pushed the disgusting scene before him back into the realm of nightmares, but his stomach remained in a knot.

A narrow path had been cleared in the garbage that covered the floor. His eyes followed the path as his heart began to race with a sick knowing that he didn't want to accept. In the far corner of the room, a body sat limply against the wall, its head hanging forward, chin rested on their chest. Long, sandy-brown hair hung in unwashed tangles, obscuring the face. Whoever this was, they'd been dragged into the room and deposited in the corner.

Taking the first, tentative step into the room, he breathed in the smell of his daughter's perfume as his mind slipped back in time to her 10th birthday party. The skating rink was full of laughing pre-pubescent girls and a few lucky guys that Caroline insisted be invited. The music was loud, the lights were flashing, and his daughter was happy. Her smiling face was forever etched in his mind in an instant of innocent joy.

His next steps brought images of Caroline and her mother, whom she looked so much like. They were trying on make-up in one of those boutique stores downtown while he was supposed to be wandering through the bookstore next door. He'd waited and watched them for half an hour before they noticed. He watched his wife impart her wisdom and techniques for putting on make-up to the next generation, the younger woman eager to learn and thankful for the knowledge. Caroline had said something funny and both of them laughed. It was one of those memories he knew he'd carry with him for the rest of his life.

She was always so witty and fun to be with, he thought, then scolded himself for using the past tense, as if she were already gone. Caroline was such a sweet soul, beautiful and compassionate. Her thirst for life was so contagious that she elevated everyone around her, just by being herself.

Standing in a room littered with trash, he wondered if he'd ever see that Caroline again. Could they ever get back to the life they had before he and his wife fought tooth and nail to just get her through high school? College was a forgotten dream. All that was before a fifty-year-old man had to get up at four a.m. to get ready to search the city's underbelly for his little girl. Before he'd learned far more about drugs than he ever wanted to know. It was before failed rehab after failed rehab. It was before his exasperated wife couldn't take it anymore and left for greener pastures that weren't pockmarked with scabs and unexplained sores. Before gonorrhea and herpes entered his life via his baby girl, and before her innocence was obliterated.

As he moved closer, he could tell the shape in the corner was a female and his heart sank deeper. His mind tried reminding him that it didn't have to be her; that it could be someone else's daughter, but his heart didn't listen. He'd found her in all kinds of conditions in all kinds of houses just like this one. Once she was completely naked, more than once she'd soiled herself, one time she'd been beaten, and gang-raped. It was all part of his reality now, whether he liked it or not. She was still his little girl and every time he'd found her. Every time he'd carried her to his car. Every time he took her to the hospital, or detox, or rehab. Every time he had found her and every time, she turned out to be okay, relatively speaking.

Kneeling before the limp form he closed his eyes and steeled himself for the discovery that awaited him as a memory began to play itself out in his mind.

"Daddy, will you read to me?" Caroline asked in her precious, innocent four-year-old voice.

"I will always read to you, sweetheart." The smile that swept across her face melted his heart. She had been a beautiful child with a vivacious laugh and blue eyes that lit up a room.

Opening his eyes, he looked at the dirty, disheveled form before him. If she wasn't his daughter, she was someone's daughter. Before him was a life in ruination, never to return. She was someone's daughter. Someone's hopes and dreams lay extinguished before him. The only question now was whose?

Reaching out with an unsteady hand, he stroked the hair atop the girl's head gently. "I'm so sorry for you," he whispered into the silence as a tear rolled down his cheek. "You deserve better."

Slipping his hand down the girl's face, he slid his fingers under her chin and slowly raised her face into view. Dropping the rag to the floor, he raked the dirty, greasy hair out of her face with his free hand. For a moment he stared into his daughter's dirty face as tears flowed down his cheeks. He was paralyzed by grief. He was too late. If he'd come here first, maybe. If he'd woken up earlier or looked harder, or...

Slipping onto his knees he cradled her into his arms, pulling her limp body against his chest. There was nothing else to do now but to hold her and love her, as he'd done her whole life. Pent-up emotion poured forth from him as he rocked her gently amid a sea of garbage cast off by countless people whose families worried just like he did. Every night spent in anguished worry poured from his eyes as tears and fell on Caroline's dirty, unwashed hair as he gently stroked the back of her head. His body began to shake with quiet sobs, and he closed his eyes, clinging to what was left of his precious child.

"I got you, baby. Daddy's here," he whispered to her. "I found you."

The Man with a Hundred Wives

The old mailbox had seen better days. Faded to a dull gray and under the assault of rust and vines, it sat tilted to one side on a post that looked like a good wind would blow over. The door hung open like the slack jaw of an idiot. The guy that lived here probably didn't get much mail.

Charles Brown looked at the paper in his hand again. Below the Youth Community Service of Hillburn County logo, there was a name and an address. His eyes went back to the battered mailbox before him. Barely distinguishable amid the briars that threatened to consume it, he found the address. 143 ½ Short Distance Road. With a heavy sigh, he turned to the home that belonged to the mailbox. He was at the right place. Unfortunately.

The old house didn't even have the benefit of looking like it had once been a beautiful home. It looked like it had always been old and lonely. Sitting on a small, overgrown lot three blocks off the road on a narrow lane filled with potholes, the house looked like an old man on life support. What little spirit and paint it might have possessed had long since deserted it.

Charles stepped off the cracked sidewalk and onto a footpath through the tangle of weeds that led him to a set of suspiciously uneven steps. The wood groaned as he mounted them like it had been a long time since they'd been used. He stood on a weathered stoop and knocked on an equally weathered door. His eyes washed over the multiple colors of paint it had worn through the years by way of the various flakes and chips that time and weather had lent it.

The old man with long gray hair and a matching beard who snatched the door open was slightly out of breath and looked like he'd been interrupted in the middle of something important. The two stood in silence and stared at one another, both absorbing the quantum leap between their appearances. He was dressed in layers of old clothes, poorly matched, and stood slightly bent beneath a long gray coat that hung open.

His eyes tucked deeply into his skull, narrowed, and peered at the young man suspiciously.

The young man, in his jeans and t-shirt, possessing the latest pseudo pompadour haircut shrank somewhat beneath the weight of the stare but didn't run away. Not that he didn't want to.

"What do you want?" the man asked in a fast-spoken sentence, almost making one word out of four.

Charles swallowed. "You signed up for community service. I'm here." He extended a hand and for the first time noticed that the paperwork was clenched in a fist. He smoothed the single sheet against his chest, then handed it to the old man.

"You are Adolphus Zanderfield, aren't you?"

The old man snatched the paper and turned slightly, holding it with both hands in a way that allowed the sunlight to fall on it. He looked the papers over with quick, exaggerated movements of his head, spending entirely too much time to peruse the short paragraph typed on it. Finally, satisfied, he turned back at the teenager standing on his stoop and his eyes narrowed again.

"That depends. Are you Charles Doodoo Brown? They said to expect you."

The kid's brow furrowed beneath the serious look the old man wore. "I'm Charles, ugh, Thomas Brown. Like it says on the paper."

"Okay Charles, ugh, Thomas Brown. What you do to get in this predicament?"

"I stole a car, robbed a bank, and killed twelve men."

The hair surrounding the man's mouth moved as he pursed his lips. "You're full of shit, Doodoo Brown. That's probably why they call you that."

"Nobody calls me that."

"Sure they do. Maybe you don't hear, but they do."

Charles shrugged, uninterested in arguing. "Whatever."

The old man bent closer to Charles, his silver-blue eyes peering at the kid through a handful of loose gray hair that had fallen over his face. His breathing was shallow and coarse like he'd smoked for a very long time. Finally, he stood, keeping his eyes on Charles.

"Are you a virgin, Doodoo Brown?"

"What?" Charles shook his head. "What does that have to do with anything?"

"A boy who's never been laid ain't got the strength to do nothing worth doing."

"I'll do just fine then." Charles looked around the yard. "Besides, it looks like you need all the help around here you can get."

The old man stood in the doorway for another moment, then threw his head back and let out a hearty laugh. It rolled from him like music; like it was permeating from every pore of his body, filling the area with the sound of it.

Charles smiled. Anybody who could produce such a joyous sound couldn't be all bad. Could he?

"Meet me around back. Gate's over there." The old man pointed to his left then closed the door hard, sending flakes of various colored paint raining onto the weathered stoop. Charles watched them flutter in the sunlight as they fell.

The slow, gentleness of their movements reminded him of a snow globe he'd had as a young boy.

After carefully navigating the steps, again, Charles found another dirt path among the weeds and followed it to the side of the house. There a tall chain-link fence was being devoured by vines. The gate, rusted beyond repair, hung half open. He paused outside the gate, taking in the spectacle of the man's private yard.

The limited viewpoint afforded him the only partial sight of the towering oak tree that dominated the whole space. Its long, arching branches created a canopy that bathed the yard an odd, dusky feel. A few bottles of different colors hung from its lower branches, swaying ever so slightly with the movement of the tree. The ground, devoid of even a blade of grass, was as hard-packed and smooth as a tile floor. Heaps of junk sat in the shade, deteriorating quietly as time marched past them.

"You coming in or just looking?"

Charles jumped and took a step back as the old man appeared in the opening before him. He watched him spin and move into the yard, then followed tentatively, shaking his head. This was either going to be the hardest, or coolest twelve hours of community service he'd done yet.

Inside the gate his view expanded considerably, revealing more bottles hung from the tree in numbers that had to range in the hundreds, creating a kaleidoscope effect in the dim sunlight. At his feet, the hard-packed earth turned into an elaborate tiled pattern stretching across the yard before fading into the tangles of junk along the entirety of the fence that surrounded the property.

A low tone resonated in his mind, gathering his attention, and directing it to his right. A small shed with a covered porch sat quietly at the far end of the yard. On the porch were two rocking chairs and a hammock.

Another low tone of a slightly different pitch washed over him, and his eyes scanned the yard for the source.

A massive wind chime hung from one of the lower limbs of the tree. The tubes ranged from eight to ten feet long and were at least a foot in diameter each. At the center, dangling beneath an ornately carved wooden clapper, a shiny piece of blue and white metal swayed gently in the breeze.

Charles reached out his hand and gingerly tilted the sail of the wind chime to afford him a better view. His eyes narrowed slightly, confirming that the metal sitting heavy in his hand was indeed a genuine Alpha Romero hubcap center emblem.

"Like that? I made it."

Charles jumped, releasing the emblem. It swung on its wire and struck one of the tubes, producing a low note that resonated through his body and across the yard. He looked around, surprised at his position. He remembered seeing the emblem from the gate, but not crossing the yard.

"Pretty cool," he replied as casually as he could.

"The piece there is intriguing. It refers to a local legend of a dragon that tormented the area and was later slaughtered by the Squire of Angera named Uberto."

"It's an Alpha Romero hubcap centerpiece," Charles said flatly.

The old man shook his head. "Yes, I suppose it is at that." He turned to walk toward the shed but stopped and faced him again. "You're going to want to be careful, Doodoo Brown, things aren't always what they appear. Open your mind, kiddo, before you miss out on some wonderful things in this life."

Charles watched the old man walk toward the shed, suddenly aware that he had a slight limp. His old, worn-out boots plodded along over the sea of elaborate tiles, sending up tiny clouds of colored dust as his footprints obliterated the artwork on the tiles.

Sweeping his own eyes down to his own feet, Charles toed the ground, scrubbing up the powder that created the design on what he thought was tile. He bent and pinched up the dust, mixing the red and blue powder on his fingertips. Had the ground been covered with tile before? Or was it just an illusion, or a mistake on his part? As he blew the powder from his fingertips, a strange dizzying sensation fell over him, like his equilibrium was suddenly off.

Or was it off before and just now fell into place?

He looked around, expecting to find the old man. His voice was close, almost in his ear, but the noises of clutter being shoved around in the shed told him that the man was still there. Had he heard the voice, or just imagined it?

Charles blew the rest of the power from his fingertips and watched it settle to the ground, wondering why anyone would go through so much trouble for something so temporary. The hours taken to create the look had to be immeasurable, but then he plodded across it like it was nothing.

"You see, young man, nothing is as simple as what we see." The old man exited the shed carrying a large piece of wood. He stabbed one end into the ground and spun it, revealing an image almost identical to the sail on the wind chimes. "This is a shield of the army of Ottone Visconti, archbishop of Angera, used on the first Crusades."

Charles rose and crossed the yard, then kneeled to look at the piece being held upright by the old man's boney hand. His fingers washed over the heavy, beautifully painted wood. His pointer finger found a deep, long gash and followed it, mesmerized by the intricate beauty of the shield and the savagery of the violence thrust upon it.

"Arise, Sir Doodoo," the old man said with a laugh.

Charles shook his head and stood quickly, taking a step back as his mind returned to itself. "What the hell?"

"What the hell what?"

Charles rubbed the back of his neck. "Nothing. it's just that…"

The old man threw his head back, again filling the air with his melodious laugh.

"It's okay, Sir Charles. Things can sometimes take a few minutes to make sense, or maybe a few years. Who knows? I'm not an expert on this stuff."

"This stuff?"

He threw his hands out, motioning to the entirety of the lot.

"All this. Everything. It's a bit much to take in." The shield fell to the ground with a heavy thud as he released it and walked toward Charles, now ten feet away.

Nothing here will harm you. Do not be afraid.

"I'm not afraid," Charles replied.

The man stopped before him and smiled. "I never said you were."

Charles forced a smile, still confused. Had the old guy said he was scared? Or did he imagine he'd said it? He heard his voice say it, but did he *say* it?

"See?" the old man asked.

Charles turned to find him forty feet away, standing at the back of the house. The weathered boards of the wall next to him were nearly covered with a wide assortment of gears and gadgets, all intricately woven together to form a tapestry of rusty metal.

"Nothing is as it appears." The old man stretched a hand out of the arm of the heavy wool coat and laid a finger against a tooth of the gear closest to him. With a slight flick of his finger, he set the small gear, not much bigger than a silver dollar, into motion. It spun on its axis for a moment, then fell against another, engaging that gear and moving it. That gear then set another into motion. The movement spread across the wall and gears, each spinning at different speeds as it engaged the gear next to it, the size of which increased with each passage of momentum.

Charles stood before the wall, his eyes following the spread of movement as each gear engaged and set the next into motion. When the trail was finished, zigzagging back and forth across the wall, a massive gear at the bottom left began to turn slowly. He stared at the massive piece of rusted metal wondering what kind of equipment it could have been taken from. A gear three feet across would surely have been housed in a monstrosity of a machine, the likes of which he'd never seen.

The sound of the gears in motion fell on him like a buzz of a million bees as metal met metal in a smooth, seamless dance. The gears, countless in numbers and size, and shades of rust filled his mind with music he'd never heard but suddenly longed to know intimately. He stood, mouth slightly agape in wonder, as the sound enveloped him, transporting him to a state of mind that lent him a peace and calm he'd never experienced before. He was everywhere, and nowhere simultaneously. He was asleep and awake, loved and in love at the same time. He existed, and he didn't.

As the movement on the wall began to slow his vision cleared and he was looking at rusty gears and weathered boards again. Drifting back from where he'd been, Charles slowly became aware of the wetness in his crotch. He moved, adjusting himself in his jeans. His first thought was that he'd wet himself, but the stickiness of the wetness told him that he had not. It was worse.

Looking around while his mind tried to come to grips with all it had experienced, he found the old man sitting next to a small collection of rocks encircling a bed of red embers near the shed. Atop the fire, perched atop a four-way lug wrench used for changing tires, sat an iron skillet. In the pan, a mixture of minced meat and chopped potatoes sizzled above the heat. A tiny flume of smoke rose from the fire, dancing along the underside of the skillet. His eyes watched as it slipped from beneath the cast iron skillet and slithered toward the bluest sky he'd ever seen.

"And he's back." The old man chuckled and pinched up a lump of the mixture on his plate with a piece of white bread and took a bite. "Have a nice trip?" he added with a smirk.

"What the hell did you do to me?" Charles asked, stomping up to the man, ignoring the flumes of colored powder settling on his expensive tennis shoes.

"I didn't do anything." The old man grabbed another bite and shoved it in his mouth. "You did all that on your own."

"You hypnotized me."

"I did nothing of the sort," the man replied with an incredulous snort.

Charles adjusted himself again. "You hypnotized me and molested me, you fucking pervert!"

The old man finished his meal and sat the plate aside before standing. "I never laid a hand on you, kiddo. You just don't wanna believe what you saw, what you did, or where you've been."

"I've been right here."

The old man shrugged. "Perhaps, perhaps not." His silver-blue eyes scrutinized Charles. "Do you believe I've spent a hundred years collecting the perfect gears and a hundred more arranging them in just the exact position so that I can get my jollies watching a sniveling punk mess up overpriced jeans?"

Charles's shoulders dropped, knowing the man was right. "No."

"Look, it's all good, Sir Charles Doodoo Brown. First time I went I peed all over myself." He went back to the fire, picked up his own plate, and dished a pile of the meat mixture onto it. He dropped a few slices of bread on top and brought it back to Charles. "Hungry?"

"Yes, I'm starving." Charles took the plate and began devouring the food with his fingers. "I just had breakfast. Don't know why I'm so hungry," he said through a mouthful of food.

"First of all, don't talk with your mouth full. It's kinda gross. Especially corned-beef hash. And secondly, you have been standing there-" he paused to look up at the sun, allowing the dappled light to fall on his face. "About three hours."

"Three-" Charles chewed and swallowed the food in his mouth. "Three hours?"

The old man chuckled. "Pretty good for the first time."

Charles joined him by the fire. "Are you a witch?"

"Really?" the old man asked, leveling his gaze at Charles. "Witches are women. Warlocks are male."

"Sorry." Charles ate the rest of his food in silence, then looked at the man again. "Are you a warlock?"

"No."

"What are you?"

"I'm an old man, can't you tell by looking at me?"

"I see you're an old man, but this place…" Charles trailed off as he surveyed the yard. "The wind chimes, the floor." He swept two fingers across the ground, gathering up some of the colored dust. He held them before him, allowing the dust to fall into the embers where it crackled noisily. Small tongues of fire leaped up, their color matching that of the powder. "And the gears on the wall."

"Pretty neat shit, ain't it?"

Charles nodded emphatically. "You think? Look, your secret is safe with me. What is this place?"

Adolphus Zanderfield shrugged. "It's my backyard."

"It's more than that and you know it."

The man shrugged again. "You seem like a good kid. My advice to you is to go away and forget about this place. I've signed your paper and given you a glowing review and a recommendation to the judge that your record be expunged. He will do it. Trust me."

"Go? Why?"

The old man sighed and slumped in his chair. "I'm tired."

"Of what?"

"Living."

"What? I don't understand."

"And that's best, for you. Go home, enjoy your life to the fullest, grow up, have kids, grow old and die and be thankful for that too."

"I don't understand. This place is awesome. I could stay here forever."

"You say that, but forever is a long time, kiddo. Be careful what you wish for."

"I haven't wished for anything. I'm just saying there is some cool stuff here." Charles ran a hand over the back of his neck to smooth the fine hairs that were beginning to rise there. He looked around the lot as the air around him slowly began to take on a charge.

"You feel it?" The old man looked to the sky as a clap of thunder rolled over them.

"It wasn't supposed to rain today."

The old man got up and moved his chair under the porch, then retrieved the skillet, putting it on a shelf. "Better get under here or more than your drawers are gonna be wet."

Charles stood and joined him, rolling his shoulders as his skin began to tingle. "I feel like I'm being shocked or something."

"It'll pass." The man surveyed his yard as the first drops of rain began to fall. The first few drops struck strategically placed pieces of junk and produced a series of pinging noises in rapid succession.

Charles watched and listened as the rain began to fall in irregular patterns, each drop finding a piece of junk that produced a different sound. In a matter of seconds, the rain turned the menagerie of junk into an eloquent symphony of beautiful sounds. He stood, enthralled, as his eyes and ears tried to discern the sounds, placing them with the once-maligned junk that the rain struck. In the end, he gave up and allowed himself to enjoy the music.

His eyes fell to the ground a few inches from his feet. The rain that fell to the ground was beginning to wash the powder into a tapestry of color. He watched as the powder, moved, and shifted by the rain, began to flow into shapes and images, creating a painting that he could only equate to the impressionist masters of Monet and Renoir.

As the music played, the swirling collage of color on the ground began to take shape, revealing a collection of women in pastel dresses and hats making their way across a field set ablaze in a riot of wildflowers of every shape and color imaginable.

"Ah. There they are," the old man said nodding his head with a smile. "I call this one, 'My Hundred Wives'. It has to be my favorite."

Charles looked from the man to the ground in amazement. "So you're seeing this too?"

"It's real," he said with a nod. "There's a lot of them that come when it rains. The music changes, the painting changes. Nothing stays the same, kiddo, but sometimes they do repeat."

Charles shook his head and extended a hand to the edge of the roof, collecting the rainwater in the palm of his hand. He looked at the clear water for a moment, then tilted his hand and allowed it to pour out.

"This place is freaking amazing and you act like it's nothing." he shook his head. "I mean, in my mind, I'm referencing impressionist painters who died in the 1800s that I've never heard of before and you're just like 'meh'."

"Oh, on the contrary, my young friend. This place is amazing, but it's just a place. It's not the lot that makes this stuff happen." He shouldered his coat higher and pulled it closed against the rain, allowing his eyes to wash over the lot.

"Then what is it? Magic?"

"It's not magic," he sighed and shook his head. "You see, I'm not as old as you think."

"How old are you?"

"Guess."

Charles scratched his chin. "I don't know. Maybe seventy-five?"

The man laughed again, adding his own music to that of the rain. "That's how old I was when I became a Keeper."

"A 'Keeper'?"

The old man nodded with a sigh. "I'm just over six hundred and fifty years old."

"Yeah, right."

"No shit. Really. Keepers live as long as they have to."

"Oooookay," Charles said, turning his eyes back to the painting on the ground before him. The crowd of women had grown, their numbers reaching almost to the gate. If he had to guess their number, he would have to put it close to one hundred.

"You see, young man. Things like art and music and wonder and joy don't just happen in this world. They are fleeting. If not for the Keepers, they would eventually evaporate or be depleted. We kinda help to create things and to keep the flow moving."

Charles stared at the old man, not wanting to believe him, but unable to dismiss him at the same time. Something inside his chest knew he was telling the truth. He looked back at the ground, watching as the colors began to run together, ruining the painting. His eyes scanned the junk as the last few notes of music played themselves out. The symphony was over, and the rusted metal was turning back into a simple collection of junk.

As the rain ended, a profound sense of sadness filled his chest and he fought back tears. The weight of a hand fell on his shoulder and a warmth began to push back against the sadness. The two stood silent until the last raindrop fell, and the sadness was gone from his body.

"I don't know what to say."

The old man chuckled. "Sometimes there is nothing that needs to be said." He lifted his hand from Charles' shoulder and quietly slid a chair behind him.

When his knees wobbled once, then buckled, Charles felt himself falling but couldn't stop it. He sat down hard on the chair. Looking around he wondered where it came from, then looked up at his companion.

"You're okay, young man. It happens." Adolphus looked down at Charles and smiled. "You see, we Keepers do a great service for humanity. We are trusted with the seeds of all that is beautiful in man, but it is a lonely job. You're only the second person to ever see this lot. The first was a very long time ago. A beautiful young woman."

"What happened to her?"

He shrugged. "She saw the gears. Imagination, you know." His mood grew cold and distant. "She stood there for three days. It was too long, but we're not supposed to pull you out. It's complicated." He shook his head and smoothed the crop of silver hair around his mouth. "Anyway, she stayed too long, and it did something to her. When she finally came out, she was different, but not in a good way. One day, years later, a newspaper got thrown over the fence there. Maybe it was a coincidence, maybe not. I don't normally take the paper, mind you, but I opened it and there she was. She was married to some big shot millionaire or something. I can't remember. All I know is that looking into her eyes I knew there was nothing beautiful within her. Not even one scrap."

"But that's not your fault. She was probably that way, to begin with."

The old man chuckled and shook his head. "It's not for me to say. I'm just a Keeper."

"So, how long do Keepers do this? Do you ever retire?"

"Not in the sense you're imagining. Some of us are over a thousand years old. Maybe older. When we feel ourselves getting depleted, we find and train a replacement, then we simply become part of the creation, a part of the fabric of beauty and art and music. I like to think I may become a gear on the imagination wall."

Charles looked back to the ground before him, now washed clean of the dust. He stared at the dull, lifeless mud and sighed, realizing the fragility of the beautiful creation that had been there. A gentle dong of the windchimes drew his attention. His eyes fell on the rusted metal of the pipes and a smile came to his lips.

"Do you know that I once got a failing grade in art class?"

"I am not surprised. Art teachers sometimes want to impose too many rules and lines on art. It's not their fault, mind you, but it's a natural reaction to something that cannot be contained."

"So, you said you were tired?"

"I'm bone-weary, young man. This place is a difficult gig. There's so much ugly, so much strife. It's hard to keep the flow open." He sighed and ran both hands over his hair. "Many years ago, the area outside this fence used to be beautiful. The whole neighborhood did. It was a glorious place back then. It all flowed out from this place and enveloped everything."

"What happened?"

He shrugged. "I don't really know. I got old and tired, then older and more tired. When I noticed the shrinking happening, I started looking for my replacement. It's not easy either, you know."

Charles thought about the rundown neighborhood, the overgrown yard, then the vines on the very fence that surrounded the yard.

"Looks to me like the wolves are at the door."

"Looks that way to me too, kiddo." He ran a hand over his beard and held it in his hand for a moment, contemplating something deeply. "As I said, it's a tough gig."

"I'm sure it is. You should probably start training your replacement."

"I was thinking about looking for one. They don't just come along. Sometimes they need to be compelled to show up."

Charles nodded, admitting that he wouldn't be here if not for the court-ordered community service. "You know, before, I really didn't rob a bank and kill people. I was just being a smartass."

"I know," he answered with a nod. "You're just a man without direction."

Charles swallowed hard. "My whole life I've felt lost until I stepped through that gate."

"I know." The old man sighed and picked up a bucket of red powder. "I've been waiting for you." He handed the bucket to Charles and picked up one containing blue powder.

"What's your favorite color?" Charles asked.

The old man bent toward Charles, peered at him as his silver-blue eyes bored into his own. He threw his head back and filled the lot with joyous laughter.

"What's so funny?"

When he finished laughing the old man shook his head. "You haven't even noticed have you?"

"Noticed what?"

The old man bent closer to Charles, opening his eyes wide. "I'm blind, genius."

Charles's mouth fell open as he stared into the man's eyes, for the first time seeing a universe of galaxies and stars, the depth of which he couldn't comprehend. He felt himself begin to waiver, almost weightless. For a moment, he was floating, but a nudge brought him back to Earth.

"C'mon," The old man said with another laugh as he straightened up. "You have a lot to learn and I only have a hundred or so years left to teach you."

I Didn't Come Here to Die

"I came here to die," said the old man in the chair next to me beneath the shade of a coconut palm, mere feet from the endless expanse of the Pacific.

Looking over at him with an exasperated sigh, I watched him watch me. His thin, silver hair was brushed straight back from his face, giving me a good look at his tanned, wrinkled skin and weary eyes. Blue, just like mine, but he had seen far more years in the sun, losing the twinkle they once had.

I wondered what had made his body so thin and frail. Disease? A hard life? Or just the fact that he'd long outlived his collagen. The old man was right about having come here to die, but then again, hadn't we all in one way or another?

Torn away on the currents of thought, I wondered if he were me in thirty years, after countless endless summers in this place. Or was I him that many years ago, before too much rum and too much sun?

There were, I surmised, worse ways to go. A warm beach with the ocean serenading you as it falls at your feet, palm fronds rustling in the breeze overhead, rum drinks being delivered by dark-skinned cabana girls in small yellow bikinis, it beats the hell out of busting your balls in an office all your life.

Cancer, my mind told me, interrupting more pleasant thoughts. It must be cancer that had consumed this old guy and brought him to the tropics to die. He'd probably escaped some Midwest state with cold winters where they grow wheat or corn or something like that. Hell, he might have been a rutabaga farmer for all I knew... or cared. The fact was that every non-native drunk bastard who lived here had a story. We all did.

Pushing the thought of an old man's demise out of my head, I laid back, my posture matching the old man's. Two bodies lying in a state of irrevocable semi-awareness of a world that only reared its ugly head on hung-over mornings when I wished I lived closer to the town where they sold aspirin on every street corner.

Though I tried mightily to keep them out, thoughts of the old man squirmed its slimy way into my mind. Opening my eyes, I spared him a glance. Was his statement drunken gibberish? Just idle talk? An ice breaker so that he could endear himself to me enough to bum a cigarette later. Sorry old man, I left that habit back in the 'States. Many more new vices occupied my time now, and a good smoke was hell to come by anyway.

"Did you hear what I said?" the old man asked, reclining, with one hand behind his head and a drink in the other.

I sipped my drink and denied to myself that I cared. I didn't want to know why he was here, and the fact that he was occupying a chair that could have been the temporary residence of any number of cute young tourists wasn't lost to me either. Better company and easier on the eyes too.

"Die if you will, old man, but leave me out of it." I watched him, but he never moved a muscle. I was here on vacation, albeit a permanent one, but a vacation, nonetheless. "The days are longer here, so you'll probably end up living longer than you thought."

Me? I've got plenty of years left. Thirty, forty years, maybe longer if I give up the rum, but that's not going to happen. Thirty years of long days and even longer nights. Ah, the nights, when the girls smell of coconut and flowers and their bodies feel warm in the darkness when the cool ocean breezes roll in with the tide.

I closed my eyes and smiled, sliding one hand behind my head while the other held my nearly empty glass, lost in the serenity of paradise.

"Death," the old man went on, although I was a terrible audience, "is just inevitable. That's the hell of it all."

Pursing my lips irritably, I wished the old man would go away. Death is inevitable, but so is the sunset. The tide rolls in, the tide rolls out. Rum ruins your liver. Shit happens. Death is the unpleasantry that comes with a life that must be overlooked for the pure ecstasy of today. Didn't you read the brochure?

"Well, if you're going to die you better drink up." Following my own advice, I lifted my glass to my lips as the smile faded from them. Damned old man. Why must you come here and ruin my day with your prophecies of death? Draining the last of the watered-down alcohol, I looked through the bottom of the glass, watching for a moment as the pacific thrashed against the beach.

I lifted my glass high - the signal for another round - and looked at the empty chair next to me. I looked down the beach for him, but I knew he wouldn't be there. The old man was the product of a mind drunk by noon, passed out by two in the afternoon, and drunk again by nine. He was a foreshadowing as constant a companion to me as the rum I learned to love so much.

"I didn't come here to die," I lied. I came here to drink and have fun. I knew I'd see him again, like it or not. He came and went like that. A ghost of a dream, or a nightmare. He was here before me, and he'll be here after the me I see in the mirror. Wherever I am, he is also, in another dance of denial that we have grown accustomed to.

This union, as strange as it is, would work out for both of us eventually. I suppose we will both get what we want in one way or another. I came here to drink and drink I would. He came here to die and die he would. Every drink I drink will kill a piece of the old man until, finally, I can't see his face.

Then, after all this time, I'll find the peace that I came here for.

The Girl who made it Thunder

Miranda Humboldt stared at the topographic map of Boonville, Alabama spread out on her kitchen table, thinking that it was even less impressive on paper. Her left hand lifted a clear overlay and placed it over the topographic map. The thin lines drawn on the overlay matched the town perfectly, depicting the streets, houses, and any building of note. Through the overlay, she traced the topographical lines of the low valley that extended from the base of a small rise on the western edge of town to the red smiley face representing city hall.

Her blue eyes followed the valley from town back to the higher land at the end of the hollow. There, she'd drawn a small circle with four lines protruding from it. Although it resembled a child's drawing of the sun, she knew it represented the town's water tower. The tower consisted of four towering hollow legs that supported a massive, round tank that held 85,000 gallons of water when full. She allowed the figures to run through her head again, for the umpteenth time. 85,000 gallons at 8.34 pounds per gallon equaled 708,900 pounds. Or just over 354 tons.

A narrow smile crept across her lips. That would do the trick, even with significant spillage. Hell, the empty tank alone would probably do what she needed it to do.

Miranda picked up a pencil, shaking it back and forth in her right hand nervously, as the left hand flipped another page onto her blueprint of destruction. A schematic drawing of their town's very own water tower laid before her. The engineering to bring it down at the exact angle without destroying it would be difficult to work out, but she had a general idea of what it would take. The two front legs would need to be buckled at the same time, causing the weight of the tank to lurch forward. Then, as it fell, the back legs would have to be detached to prevent them from stopping its movement down the hollow.

Then, 'The Orb of Death'- no. She didn't want to kill anybody. 'The Orb of Destruction' would be free to roll with the natural terrain, cross over Hobson Street and slam into the front doors of city hall. Between the weight and the momentum, it would roll right over the hypocrisy and indignation that this piss ant town loved to dish out to people who did not toe their line.

A moment of indecision swept over her. This was all crazy. It was going too far. It was too far-fetched to work. She'd probably just end up in jail, and for what? Because they wouldn't grant her a business license?

She shook her head, clearing her doubt. Things were going on in this town that shouldn't go on. The whole town was controlled by a few people who had money. The Boons. They walked around like they owned the place, sticking their noses into everything anyone ever did.

All she wanted was to open a little shop and sell her artwork, her photographs, and a few trinkets. The faces staring back at her at the city council meeting when she petitioned for a business license looked at her with such judgment and righteous indignation that it made her stomach roll. Yes, she answered, some of her photographs contained nude models-herself included. But they were tastefully done and were not graphic. No, she did not consider herself an exhibitionist. No, she did not see the potential implications. No, she didn't think she was contributing to the moral decay of the town.

No, you can't have a license.

The image of the tight-lipped gray-haired woman sitting behind the Ms. Boon nameplate swam into her mind and she snapped the pencil in her hand. The woman, who had to be pushing 70, wouldn't recognize art if it hit her in the face.

Shaking the memory from her head, she tossed the broken pencil onto the plans and stood. All the information thus far had been readily available on the internet, but a working knowledge of measured explosives had her stumped. The best way to execute the plan was small charges, either set to a timer or set off remotely, but setting it up properly would be impossible unless she could find the knowledge and the explosives.

Or someone who would help her, someone she could trust.

Miranda got out of her car and shielded her eyes from the sun as she surveyed the farmland before her. Sweeping across the rows of waist-high corn, she looked to the west and found the pale blue water tower. It was situated on the far edge of the field, surrounded by a chain-link fence. The hulking metal structure looked out of place and ugly among the mature hardwoods that lined the edge of the small plateau.

"Looking for something in particular?"

Miranda turned with a smile, recognizing the voice.

Anniston Rainier had a reputation of being hard to read, having survived a war in the desert and a lifetime of farming, but he was partial to Miranda. When he came into the hole-in-the-wall diner where she waited tables, he was always friendly with her and left a big tip. She always took the time to listen to him and made sure his coffee or sweet tea was topped off. He was a nice man, probably lonely, and like most older men, he enjoyed flirting with young women he didn't have a chance in hell of getting.

"There you are, Mister Rainier." Miranda went to the porch of the modest farmhouse and climbed the steps.

"What do I owe the pleasure of this visit from such a pretty girl like you?" He smiled and waved a hand at the rocking chair next to him, inviting her to sit. "I didn't forget to pay my bill, did I?"

"No sir, you didn't." Miranda sat in the rocking chair, crossing her legs at the knees. She caught his gaze as it washed over the long, tanned legs that protruded from her cut-off denim shorts. "I guess this is a social call."

"Dam. Wish I'd known. I'd cleaned myself up." He laughed, running a hand over his salt and pepper hair. "Want a beer? It's good and cold." He reached into the cooler next to him and pulled out a bottle of Bud Light, offering it to her. It wasn't her brand, but Miranda took it.

"How you doing, Mister Rainier?"

"Not worth a shit, honestly. Leg's been acting up." He rubbed his right leg, which ended at the knee. It was a parting gift from the Taliban at the end of his second tour. It happened while dismantling an explosive device for the U.S. Marines and it cost him half a leg and the last two fingers on his right hand, but he'd gotten a medical pension and free care at the VA over in Souls Harbor, so the government considered it a wash.

"So about usual?" she asked with a laugh.

"Pretty much," he agreed, laughing himself.

Out of the corner of her eye, Miranda watched the man's eyes wash over her legs again. She had nice legs and she knew it and didn't mind them being appreciated. She drank half her beer as they watched the sun go down, waiting for the opportunity to broach the subject of her visit.

"Look at that shit."

Miranda looked at him, then followed his gaze. He was looking at the water tower.

"Kinda ugly, wouldn't you say?" she asked, not believing her luck.

"Ugly as hell. All of June and July the sun sets right behind it. I like to sit out here and drink a few beers and watch the sunset. Damned thing ruins the view."

"I couldn't agree more." She took a long drink of beer and pointed the bottle at the water tower. "Yep. A monstrosity is exactly what it is."

"You know the county come up here back then and poked around. Daddy ran 'em off twice but they brought the Sheriff. Said he had to let 'em survey. 'Imminent Domain' is what they called it."

"For the greater good," she echoed sarcastically, shaking her head.

"My ass. There was only two suitable places for it. Those damned Boons didn't want it on their property, so they had the bastards put it on ours."

Miranda nodded in agreement and drank from her beer as she stretched her legs out before her, crossing them at the ankles.

"Know what my dad did with the money?"

"What?" she asked, bracing herself for a tale.

"Donated it to the asshole running against Hector Boon for mayor. And the sumbitch won!" Anniston Rainier laughed loudly. "You should have seen the faces of those damned bunch of Boons."

"I hate them. Especially Felicia Boon. She's head of the city council, you know."

Anniston grunted. "I remember her. She always was a tight assed prude. She wasn't bad-looking back then, mind you, and her folks had money."

"You ever hit that?" Miranda asked with a laugh.

"Me? Hell no. She's a good bit older than me." He took a sip of beer and conceded, "Not to say I wouldn't have."

Miranda shook her head. "Well, she's got a stick up her butt now. They turned down my bid for a license for my shop."

The old man settled into his chair and shook his head. "I don't doubt it. If it weren't sanctioned by the Baptist Association, she'd turn down a hat shop."

"I've shown you my work. Definitely not sanctioned by the church. Not in public anyway."

He nodded in agreement and took a long drink of beer. "That why you're here?"

"In a way. I think I have a solution to both our problems."

"You ain't even gotta say it." Anniston stared at the young woman looking back at him, wishing for thirty years of his youth back. When she got out of her car, legs first, he knew his boring routine was about to disappear. According to the doctor, it would disappear in a few months anyway. He didn't have a long time before the cancer in his guts progressed to the point that he'd need to be in a hospital, and he couldn't think of a better way to use it than spending time with a beautiful, young woman. Even if all she let him do was look.

"You don't even know what it is."

"I'm pretty sure it's big. You got a little tank top on and those cut-off shorts showing your legs like that. You didn't pull the big guns out for nothing."

Miranda smiled and arched an eyebrow, wondering how far was she willing to go to see her plan through? When the prudish look on Felicia Boon's hawkish face swam into her head, she got her answer.

"Then we better get to work. Tomorrow is June first. We barely got a month."

After spending twenty-six evenings with Anniston Rainier, her training almost complete, Miranda stood before a ladder tied to a tall, straight pine and looked upward. She'd made the climb many times, but today the small lump in her hand wasn't play-dough, but C-4 plastic explosive. Her free hand went to the front pocket of her well-worn jean shorts, finding the remote detonator. Even with Anniston's old war connections, they could only afford enough for one real test run and the actual event. If anything went wrong with either, they were screwed.

She looked at the man next to her, the man who had taught her so much, not only about explosives. About the simple beauty of life, about the hells of war, about how to grow corn. Smiling, she remembered his patience with her eagerness, his calm with her exuberance. In many ways they were opposites, but they were similar in more ways than she could have ever guessed.

"Up you go," Anniston said, leaning on a crutch at the base of the ladder.

Miranda sighed and started up the ladder. A few steps up, she felt Anniston's hand on her butt. Pausing, she turned to look over her shoulder at him.

"Do guys ever grow out of that?" she asked with a smile.

"If a man passes up the opportunity to pat a pretty girl on the butt, he's not to be trusted," he said as a grin slid across his face.

Miranda rolled her eyes playfully and shook her head. "You something else, Anniston Rainier."

"You something else too, Miss Humboldt. Something else indeed." He watched her climb the ladder and smiled.

She climbed slowly, still smiling. Anniston had turned out to be more of a gentleman than she expected. She figured she'd have to sleep with him at least a few times, but he hadn't pushed the argument. He had asked her to cook him a meal of fried pork chops, turnip greens, fried potatoes and onions, and cornbread and then eat with him, but that was the furthest he asked her to go. Outside of a few pats to her backside, he hadn't laid a finger on her.

Miranda learned that his disdain for the town and many of the same people in it ran as deeply as hers, but for different reasons. The man, just over fifty and almost twice her age had become her friend and several things about him surprised her. Anniston was, on a good day, a kind-hearted man who gave generously of his gardening efforts to the county's food bank. On a bad day, he was angry and bitter about the lot he'd received in life. He read voraciously, including all the masters, but also enjoyed the Sunday comics. He read and wrote poetry that was quite good if sometimes a little dark. A few of the poems he'd shown her were positively heartbreaking. He'd found and married the love of his life only to lose her when he returned from the war with less than he'd left with. He both loved and hated farming, and although he hadn't said it aloud, he longed for genuine companionship.

There was more to Anniston Rainier than most people thought.

Miranda reached the top of the ladder and looked down at the man thirty feet below her. She gave him a thumbs up and went to work. She pressed the explosive onto the tree bark and secured it by wrapping a length of duct tape around it and the tree. She took out the blast control unit, switched it on, and pressed it into the lump of gray clay that stuck out above the tape.

When she reached the ground after the last one, her legs burning slightly and her hands sticky from pine resin, she joined Anniston as he stared up at her work.

"Pretty good. Not the fastest I've seen, but you did good."

"The legs of the tower are taller, but there's a walkway beneath it. I won't have to climb up but once."

Anniston nodded as he stared at the trees. He turned to her and smiled. "Let's blow some shit up."

Miranda let out an excited "Whoop whoop!" as they headed to his old truck.

After retreating a hundred yards, he turned the truck so they could watch the damage. Producing two AA batteries, a sly grin broke out on his unshaven face. He handed them to Miranda.

"Keep the batteries out until after you're clear. Remember that. I'd hate to think of your pretty little body blown all over Hillburn County. I'm serious, Miranda."

Miranda nodded, taking them, and eagerly placing the batteries in the detonator. She switched it on just like he'd shown her many times and held it out. "You ready?"

"This is your show," he said, sweeping a hand toward the trees.

Miranda looked down at the small, rectangular, metal block with one button and a toggle switch. Just above them, a red light blinked at her, sending her heartbeat into overdrive. It was the best she'd felt in a long time; excited, happy, grateful, and a little scared. The adrenaline coursing through her felt good. She'd never felt so alive.

"Here goes." She pressed the button, watching as both treetops closest to them exploded simultaneously. Two balls of fire erupted before them, sending a shower of splinters down the trunk. The top of the tree on the right fell forward and somersaulted toward the ground. The left one flipped once in the air and caught fire on the way down.

Miranda's eyes widened as she watched the fire engulf the treetop as it fell. It hit the ground and threw up a cloud of ash and embers.

"Don't lose focus, missy," Anniston told her, dampening her enthusiasm a bit as she sat next to him. "Imagine the tower pitching forward now that its legs are gone. This is the variable that will be all up to you. It has to lean forward enough to fall in the right direction. Too soon and it drops where it is. Too late and it might change the trajectory."

Miranda took in a deep breath and visualized her goal, then flipped the switch to the second frequency and pressed the bottom. The back two trees exploded like the first. She looked over at Anniston Rainier and found him smiling.

"That's gonna make one hell of a mess," he said, looking at the trees.

"Good."

"Some folks might get killed."

"We've done gone over this. That's why I'm doing it when I am. Nobody's even going to be in town, much less down at city hall."

Anniston shrugged as he adjusted his position behind the wheel of his truck. "Look, the main thing I learned in the Corps was to make your plan the best you can and execute said plan. Variables happen. Shit goes wrong, but you adapt and continue on the mission."

Miranda nodded in agreement as she fiddled with the detonator. "Do you think I'm some kinda crazy lady for doing this?"

Anniston chuckled. "Who the hell is to say what crazy is and what crazy ain't." He looked at her and smiled. "Besides, whoever said you were a lady?"

She pushed him playfully while they both enjoyed a laugh.

"Seriously, though. Sometimes I think the whole thing is nuts."

"Oh, I don't know, Miranda. If people didn't do crazy shit now and again, nothing would ever change. Sometimes, unexpected things in life end up being the things we remember when we're laying on our deathbeds."

"I can't thank you enough for all you've done."

Anniston shrugged. "You have done plenty."

Miranda shook her head, her eyes narrowing as she looked at him. "I don't get you; you know that. I mean, lotta men would have had me naked and doing all sorts of stuff, but you didn't. Why not?" She watched him shrug and turn to look out his side window. "Are you secretly gay?"

He laughed. "Dam girl, no. You're the best-looking thing I've seen in a long time. If I were a younger man and had two good legs, I'd chase you 'till I talked you into marrying me and I'd keep you in bed." He shook his head and looked back to the broken treetops as his smile faded.

"The way I see it, you're in a tight spot," he continued. "You've got no power or clout in this town. No family. Hell, I don't even know why you stay. But folks have been taking advantage of you. I hear men at the diner saying stuff, propositioning you, and you just dismiss it. The folks on the city hall won't let you open your shop because they don't want anyone to change anything. They're probably afraid their husbands will be in there looking at you and come home to them and be disappointed."

"What does that have to do with anything?"

"Point is folks been taking advantage of you. If I made you do the things that my dirty old mind has thought of, I wouldn't be any better than them. I guess patting you on the ass and having you cook supper might fit into that too, but it ain't much." He paused for a moment, considering his words. "I ain't got long left, Miranda. The doctors done told me that." He held up a hand to calm her as she opened her mouth to speak.

"But I've had a good life, albeit shorter than I expected. Admittedly it's been lonely some these last few years, but I've survived. The thing is, when I'm up at the hospital, laying in that bed, I wanted someone to think about. My memories of a lot of people have faded so that I don't know how much is real and how much ain't. I got a lot of memories of things I want to forget." He sighed and rubbed his chin. "What you've given me is some fresh memories. The look of long, toned legs. The feel of a beautiful woman's butt in my hand. The taste of a home-cooked meal. Those memories are worth a lot to me."

Miranda smiled at him then leaned across the truck, hugging him. "You're a good man, Anniston Rainier. Do you know that?"

He smiled, enjoying the embrace. "Well, don't be spreading that around too much. Folks will be wanting to talk to me and shit."

Miranda sat on her bed wrapped in a towel, another holding her wet hair, and stared at the detonator. In less than twenty-four hours the plan she first concocted almost a year ago would come to fruition, thanks to Anniston Rainier.

A sad smile crept to her lips as she thought of him, sitting on his porch alone. He'd spent a month of the few he had left helping her and had asked so little in return. Although gruff at times, he had a certain gentlemanly charm that appealed to her. He made her feel special. Of course, he wanted to sleep with her but restrained from blackmailing her into it. She would have complied, and they both knew it. He could have had her more than once in exchange for all he'd done, but he never treated her like a whore. If anything, he showed her respect, kindness, and understanding. He probably thought her plan was nuts, but never spoke it.

She flicked the toggle switch back and forth in her hand while she considered a decision. He was a nice man that had gone out of his way to help her. He deserved more memories than turnip greens and a pair of legs. She tossed the detonator onto her bed and stood. She had some work to do.

Anniston Rainier watched the headlights turn off the highway from his usual perch in his rocking chair. They wound their way along his half-mile driveway and ended up at his front porch. He shielded his eyes from the lights and asked who was there.

When the headlights died, he rubbed his eyes, allowing them to readjust to the dark. As his vision cleared, he found Miranda standing by her car wearing a long trench coat and holding a picnic basket.

"Grab us an old blanket and meet me in the back yard. Time for you to see some stars."

"What? Why you got that coat on? It's hotter than hell."

"You're right. To hell with the picnic." Miranda walked up the stairs and dropped the basket by the front door. Facing him, she unbuttoned the coat and let it fall to the weathered floorboards. She stood before him completely naked for a moment, then opened the screen door.

She looked back at him through the screen with one eyebrow cocked seductively. "You coming inside or you just gonna keep feeding the bugs?"

Driving through town, Miranda took in the spectacle that was the Fourth of July in Boonville. The town, decked out in red, white, and blue, was abuzz with excitement. Everyone was outside, either grilling meat, playing some kind of sport, or just hanging out. Many folks were enjoying adult beverages, of course, they were well disguised as to not draw the ire of the fine Christian townsfolk. For many, the day would be filled with festivities and family fun. For some, like Anniston Rainier and herself, the day would be less relaxing.

By the time the sun began to sink into the western sky, many people would begin making their way toward Fred and Sonia Boon's estate, where the whole town would be treated to a tremendous fireworks show, culminating with Fred and Sonia singing the national anthem as a duet to a crescendo of colorful explosions. It was the biggest show in town, but if things went according to her plan it wouldn't be this year.

The metal of the ladder was still warm from the day's heat, making the palms of her hands sweat more than they already were. As Miranda climbed slowly, her heartbeat increased with each rung. She'd dreamed of this for a year. She'd trained for this. Now, all she had to do not was not chicken out.

"Four balls of the dough, a roll of duct tape, four blasting caps, and the detonator." Miranda nodded. She had everything she needed. This was it. It was now or never. She continued her climb, going over the plan as she went. "Press the dough firmly to the interior surface of the metal. Secure dough firmly with duct tape, but do not cover completely. Apply both caps marked A on two legs toward town and turn on. Place two caps marked B on the other two. Turn on. Evacuate as quickly as possible. Move to a range of no more than a two-minute brisk walk, but close enough to see the target. Move the toggle to A, press the button. When ready, move the toggle to position B and press the button."

Reaching the platform quicker than she thought, Miranda climbed over the railing and spared a moment to take in the view. The town, bathed in twilight, looked like any other small town. They all had their politics and their own "royal family". It wasn't a bad place to live, but it wasn't a good one either.

She turned away from town and looked over the farmland behind her. The countless acres of pastureland and massive garden led to a small farmhouse set half a mile off the highway. A yellow rectangle of light shined in the semi-darkness. His kitchen window.

Her eyes went to the front porch. He was in his chair when she passed, but was he there now rooting for her? Did he decide to turn in early to avoid the whole scene? She felt a tug within her to be sitting on the porch with him, drinking a beer and waiting for the fireworks. They would have a nice view, with the bigger ones going off just above the trees. A smile came to her lips as she admitted that it wouldn't be a bad life, but it faded when she remembered that he was sick.

She lifted a hand and waved, knowing that he couldn't see her in the growing darkness even if he was there and watching. He was probably the best person in this whole damn town, and he wasn't going to be around much longer. The whole situation was just one giant pisser. She wished she'd met him before and known him longer. He was the kind of man that a woman could love deeply while also having to defend him from her friends who thought him an ass.

Miranda forced her mind back to the task at hand with a heavy sigh. She made her way toward the front of the tower, toward town. Using the light from her phone, she opened the small bag slung over her shoulder and took out the C-4. She pressed it to the pale blue steel and made an X of two strips of duct tape over it. She found one of the caps marked A and pushed the prongs into the top of the dough, then used a fingernail to flip the tiny switch on. The red light atop the charge came on and she smiled.

"One down, three to go." Crossing between the two front legs, she watched as the crowd began to gather at the Boon's Estate. Half the town was there already, congregating in groups on the expansive front lawn. Many had brought blankets and were staking claim to the best spots. The other half would be there shortly. She had some time before the big finale.

A moment of doubt crept into her as she set the second charge, but she talked her way through it. By the time she had the third charge set, she was over it completely. To her, the notion that the punishment had to fit the crime was preposterous. They had rejected her art and her livelihood. They looked down on a lowly waitress and told her no as if she were a child. They did it because they knew they could. No one would ever speak up. No one would ever talk back. Until now.

When the red light came on for the fourth charge, the sun had set, and the tower was dark. Miranda felt her way back to the ladder and clambered over the rail. She found the ladder and began her descent. When the first report of the fireworks went off, she let out an involuntary yelp, sure that one of the charges had gone off prematurely. More reports came, followed by bursts of red, white, and blue fireworks. The show had started at the Boon estate. She gathered herself, wiped her sweaty palms on her tee-shirt, and climbed down the ladder.

The ground felt good beneath her feet, solid and secure. She dug her phone out of the bag and checked that the toggle on the detonator was flipped up, in the A position. She shoved the phone deep in her back pocket and walked away from the tower. All that was left to do was turn the detonator on and press the button. It was almost over. Or it was about to begin? Both felt appropriate.

She walked the hundred yards to her car and leaned against the hood. The initial plan was to wait for the finale, but she knew she couldn't wait. If she did it now, there might be people still in town, but it would also rob the Boons of their big show and possibly spare the people of their horrible duet.

She smiled to herself. Yes, she'd go ahead and do it. Everyone would be there by now anyway. Even if they weren't, no one would be downtown. Not at this time of night.

Miranda inhaled deeply and blew the air out through puckered lips. "Let's do this," she said aloud. She flipped the switch on the detonator and held it out before her, gripping it tightly in her sweaty palms. Her heartbeat thundered in her ears as the fireworks appeared over the trees to her right, lighting up the sky. A smile slid across her lips as her thumb slid over the button, finding it in the dark. She pressed it, her wide eyes staring at the tower.

When nothing happened, she looked down at the remote. "What the hell?" she asked, banging it against her palm. "Oh no. I screwed it up." She flipped the switch off and on again, then extended the detonator toward the tower, pressing the button repeatedly. "No, no, no," she said. "No. Don't mess up. Dammit!"

"You remembered one important thing but forgot another."

Miranda turned and watched Anniston crutch his way up to her in the dark. "You might need these." He held out a hand, revealing two AA batteries as a series of color explosions lit up the sky.

"Oh my God! I'm such an idiot." Miranda ran to him and threw her hands around his neck. "You're my hero."

"Well, if I'm going to be an accomplice, might as well earn my bacon." Anniston smiled as he watched her place the batteries in the detonator. "But you might wanna get on with it. The show's building to the climax." Leaning on his crutch, he nodded toward the sky behind her as it erupted in red, white, and blue explosions. "I knew you wouldn't wait 'till the end."

Miranda switched the detonator on and smiled when the red blinking light appeared. She spared Anniston a brief look, then pressed the button.

Ahead of them, the darkness erupted with two red fireballs. The sound of the explosions rolled across the land in a wave, followed immediately by the low groan of metal giving way as the two front legs of the tower fell. The huge tank of the tower lurched forward for an instant, then paused.

Panic flooded Miranda's chest, but Anniston's hand on her shoulder and his soft reassurance calmed her.

"Easy. Give it a minute."

Miranda held her breath, not exhaling until the groan of metal started again. This time it was a low vibration that moved out from the tower like a song. It reminded her of the low, threatening growl of a very big dog as the feel of it passed through her. A shudder ran up her spine as the tower began to move again, the ominous sound piercing the night.

The sound, as big as a clap of thunder swept across the town, gathering the attention of everyone on the Boone's front lawn. If she'd been in a position to see it, Miranda would have witnessed a sudden shift in the crowd as they all turned, almost simultaneously, toward the tower. With their eyes wide and their mouths hung agape, they showed no interest in the fireworks lighting up the sky behind them.

"Make sure it's going where you want it." Anniston's voice was calm and soothing, reminding Miranda of the training. She threw a glance and a nervous smile at him, glad that he was here. If not, she would have panicked and blown the second charge already. She stepped sideways, putting a shoulder against his.

"There it goes, sweetheart."

The metal began to scream as the weight of the unsupported ball of water pulled it forward and downward. The fall was leading it to the hollow that led directly toward town. Just before the blue globe adorned with the word "Boonville" struck the ground, Miranda blew the second set of charges. The force of the explosion detached the two back legs and pushed the tank of the tower toward the town whose name it bore.

Miranda raced forward as the sky began to fill with the light of the big finale. She made it close enough to the edge of the rise to see the huge metal ball tumble down the hollow, taking anything in its path with it. The flash of fireworks illuminated it as it rolled, collecting speed.

Her eyes widened as it neared Hobson Street. Out of the corner of her eye, she noticed a car driving along the road toward the tank. She plotted the approach of each, hoping they wouldn't meet.

"Stop, you idiot," she pleaded. "Don't you see it?"

When the driver slammed on the brakes, bringing the car to a screeching halt, she breathed a sigh of relief, but couldn't suppress a laugh. What the hell must the driver be thinking, she wondered, as the monstrosity that used to be the town water tower hopped the sidewalk and rolled across Hobson Street twenty feet in front of the car, spewing water from several gaping holes as it went.

Her eyes followed the giant orb as it crossed the street, rolled over several parking meters, and moved across the expansive lawn of the Boonville city hall. It left a deep crevasse in the manicured lawn before slamming directly into the two-story antebellum home that housed City Hall. The front of the building offered little resistance, crumbling on impact. The water tank penetrated the home with ease, collapsing the roof and rolled over the rest of the building in two revolutions.

Miranda gasped as it moved beyond City Hall, leaving little more than a pile of rubble. Never in her wildest dreams did she imagine it would roll over the building and keep going. She didn't want to destroy the whole town or even part of it. Her beef was with city hall.

She clasped her hands to her mouth as the ball of metal rolled across the back lawn of City Hall and headed for a row of shops she frequented, including the shop that she'd tried to open. Helpless to do anything but watch, she grabbed both sides of her head and cringed.

The bulbous water tank, not completely spherical, wobbled on its axis and slowly began to shift direction. It tottered toward the bookstore across the street with an uneven movement as the water inside shifted back and forth, spewing forth when it found an opening.

A loud, grinding noise rose to meet her as the tank met Second Avenue and metal met asphalt. It struck the pole of a streetlight and shifted direction slightly again, barely catching the edge of the bookstore. Bricks tumbled to the street behind it as the authorities in town were first becoming aware of what was happening.

Two police cars converged on Hobson Street at the site of what used to be city hall while another rolled down the street behind the tank, lights, and sirens blaring. Miranda looked to her right, where throngs of people were hurriedly making their way back to downtown.

"Time to go, sweetheart."

Miranda's hand absently waved at the destruction below as she turned back to face Anniston. "It's still going."

"It appears that we've miscalculated the weight and speed of the tank, my dear," he said, a smile tugging at the corners of his mouth.

"You think?" Miranda asked through an incredulous laugh.

"Well, we better not be standing here when the shock begins to wear off and they come up here to see what the hell happened. Especially with a detonator in your hand."

Miranda's mouth fell open as the realization began to sink in. She shook her head and looked back toward the town. The tank rolled over two cars parked on the street, knocked down another light pole, and slammed into a massive oak tree on the corner of Fourth and Fifth Avenue. The tree shook from the mighty blow but held firm. The seams on the tank already stressed beyond their limits, split open, as thousands of gallons of water began pouring from the gaping wounds of the massive tank.

"Miranda."

She turned to look at Anniston again. "Now what?" she asked numbly.

He held out his hand to her and motioned her to him. "We have to go."

"Where?" she asked.

"Anywhere but here."

Miranda spared the town one last look, following the path of destruction. Except for the chimney and part of the western wall, City Hall was in ruins, cars were flattened, and water was beginning to flood downtown. Her eyes followed a policeman as he sloshed after his patrol car which was being carried down the street by the water rushing from the tank.

"Dam," she said with a chuckle of disbelief. "I didn't think it would actually work."

"It worked alright. C'mon, I could use a drink. How about you?" He turned as she joined him and started toward his house. "I think it's going to be a long night."

Miranda rested her below on the armrest of the rocking chair and laid her palm in her hand, looking at the man beside her. Her mind was reeling as fast as her heart was beating in her chest.

"I can never thank you enough."

"For what? Getting you thrown into prison?" Anniston laughed. "You may cuss me by the time you get out."

"I'm not in jail yet." Miranda lifted her beer and took a long drink. "You know you'll forever be my hero." She threw him a playful wink.

"Well, that's something I think I'd like." Anniston drank from his beer and lifted his eyes toward the road as the sound of a siren began to wail. "They'll be here in a minute."

"So," Miranda said with a shrug, "it's not illegal to sit on your porch and watch the fireworks is it?"

Anniston snorted a laugh. "I don't suppose it is." His eyes went to the police cruiser as it slowed on the road and slid into his driveway. "Not yet anyway."

"You know something? You're the best man that has ever been in my life. Better than my daddy even."

"That's a little bit sad but thank you."

Miranda watched the police car bounce over the driveway as it sped toward them. For the first time, fear began to creep into her chest as the prospect of going to jail became very real.

"I don't want to go to jail, Anniston."

He reached out and took her hand. "I know you don't, Miranda." He pulled his hand back and sat in the darkness, watching as the police car slid to a stop at the base of what was left of the water tower. "We got the fact that these cops are pretty damned stupid on our side."

Miranda smiled. "I don't regret a thing."

"Me either." Anniston stood and slid a crutch under his arm as he stood before her. He extended his free hand to her and she took it. "We better go inside. Our story of not seeing anything will be more believable."

"We got time," she said quietly. "I'm really starting to like the view from your porch."

The Finger of God

One of the things I remember most clearly is that the lightning came so suddenly and unexpectedly no one knew exactly what happened for a good five to ten seconds. Everyone sat, stunned, their eyes on the field before us like statues, and I was no exception. I was, however, looking at the right spot at the right time to see something that changed my life forever.

I'm sure most of the crowd was following the action as Dereck moved the ball down the field, badgered by a feisty, but smaller player from the Hilton County team. They were a very good team and everyone on my side of the stands, the home side, were excited to be up on them two goals to one. But I wasn't watching Dereck, I was watching Brett Wills. He was a tall, well-built, defenseman with wavy sandy brown hair and dreamy blue eyes. I couldn't tell if his eyes were dreamy from where I sat, but my teenage daughter swore to the fact. I was watching him and admitting to myself that he was a good-looking kid when the strike happened.

The forecast I'd gotten from the petite blonde on television that morning was partly cloudy with a chance of scattered showers later in the day. I was thankful for the cloud cover because, without it, the heat would have been downright miserable. Growing up in the south my sports allegiance was to college football, baseball, and basketball, in that order. Soccer was a new sport to me, and I didn't understand a bit of it. Neither did my daughter, but she was a cheerleader, and this was a school sporting event, thus she had to be here. But that wasn't the only reason.

I didn't love soccer, but I loved my daughter, so I came to watch her. Thankfully, she and the other cheerleaders were on the opposite end of the field when the lightning hurtled down from the endless gray sky as if thrown by God himself. She was far enough away, to be safe from the effects of thousands of volts of electricity slamming into the earth. Not everyone was so lucky.

For me, the milliseconds-long strike lasted a lot longer. It was as if everything slowed to super slow motion. The bolt reached down from the heavens in a bright finger and touched Brett first. It connected with his right shoulder and he froze. His face was a mixture of excruciating pain and what the hell happened? For an instant he stood motionless with this long finger of God tapping on his shoulder, then the flash connected him with a teammate, Carson - I can't remember his last name - in a glowing arch. It didn't go straight from one to the other but leaped in a smooth crescent and fell on Carson's left arm. He froze as well, just like Brett. Two teenage boys, in the prime of their lives suspended in time by one of the strongest forces of nature. It was a sight that I see often when I close my eyes, whether I want to or not.

From Carson, the lightning sprang at an angle and hit a kid from the Hilton County team just as he stopped and turned to see what was happening behind him. I think this was about the time that everyone else also tore their eyes from the action and looked back down the field and saw the flash. The bolt didn't arc from Carson to the other kid, but rather shot from his fingertips and enveloped him, almost as if he were a wizard from one of the movies that are so popular with kids about as old as the ones on the field.

That was when Brett, finally released from the grip of the electricity, fell to the ground. Just as he was hitting the grass, Carson was released and he collapsed as well, his right hand already a blackened, bloody mess. The kid from Hilton

County stood a moment longer, convulsing as the power surged through his body, but then he too fell.

The clap of thunder rolled across us all with an almost palpable sense of authority.

The crowd erupted in a mixture of fear for their own safety, and concern for the boys. The coaches were rushing onto the field, ushering the boys to safety, and calling for help for the three kids lying on the grass. People panicked and were running in every direction, crying, and screaming like they had been struck. Something inside my heart told me that my daughter was fine, so I fought the crowd and went onto the field to help. Although it had been ten years since my last run, I was still an EMT at heart.

Maybe it was because my daughter thought he had dreamy eyes, maybe it was the proximity, but the first kid I got to was Brett. He was sitting up with the aid of two parents and looked stunned, but otherwise okay. I remember the smell of his hair. It wasn't singed, but it smelled hot; like someone had thrown a bottle of Axe into a campfire. A bright red ring of blistered skin hung around his neck where his gold chain had been. Amid the chaos, my mind paused to wonder if guys still wore necklaces anymore. Brad did or had. The chain was gone and would never be found again, but it had left him with one hell of a reminder of its presence, not that he'd ever forget.

Over the noise and chaos, I heard someone begin to scream. It was a shrill, painful cry of a badly wounded young man. I didn't have to look around to know who it was. The kid, Carson, who had his fingers blown off by the lightning had awakened and began to realize his pain.

Standing, I saw a tall red-haired girl fighting frantically to push through the crowd. I edged my way through the confused bodies and took her hand. She hugged me briefly, then turned her attention to Brett. A pang of jealousy stabbed my heart, but I let it go. She was a teenager and the dreamy-eyed Brett had just been struck by lightning. I turned with a heavy sigh and looked at the screaming kid. There were several people around him and the ambulance team - required to be at every match - was already administering aid.

That was two boys accounted for. The third one, the one from Hilton County, was surrounded by a kneeling group of people, including his teammates. Someone somewhere was restraining his mother. I could hear her plaintive cries as she called out his name, but I couldn't see her for the ever-growing crowd.

The kneeling group was stunned to silence. Some were praying, some just stared in disbelief. Many of the players were holding hands and weeping openly. The third player struck by the lightning was motionless on the ground beneath a crisp, clean, white sheet. The sight of the rectangle of white cotton against the dark green grass seared itself into my brain as my heart sank. There wasn't anything me or anyone else could do for him now.

The Hilton County kid, whose name I came to learn was Avery Wheeling, was the ground the lightning was looking for. With nowhere else to go, it coursed throughout his body, frying his brain, and stopping his heart almost simultaneously before surging through all ten of his toes, rupturing the ends, and dissipating into the ground. People claimed that the surge blew the ends of his soccer cleats off, but I never saw them and didn't want to. Some of the other kids later claimed to feel the static in the air, and a few said they felt a tingling in their feet, but there was no way to be sure. Either way, it really didn't matter.

The funeral was a few days later and was one of the biggest crowds of people I had ever seen in my life, outside of a sporting or concert venue. Most of the young people from both towns attended, whether they knew the dead kid or not. It was the second saddest thing I've ever seen.

Three young men had been struck by lighting and one was dead. They made the news across the country for a few days, then the world moved on to another tragedy and they were forgotten. But the people there that day, especially me, would take the sights and sounds, the smells, and feelings of that day to their graves. Whether it was a "rogue lightning strike", the hand of God, or just bad luck, one instant lasting only a millisecond had changed all our lives forever, in one way or another.

In the days and weeks following "the rouge lightning strike" everyone suddenly became experts on lightning and its effects on the human body. You'd hear hushed conversations in restaurants, pick up on key words like "electromagnetic impulse" and "amperage" when passing small groups on the sidewalk. It was a small town. Not much else to talk about I suppose.

Brett was lucky, he was just a conduit, left with some minor nerve and muscle damage that his therapists would fix by Christmas. Carson caught the energy that passed through Brett, but by then it was looking for a ground. It passed through his left arm, his chest, and exited his right arm, blowing off three of his fingers and burning the hell out of his hand and forearm. The doctors were concerned about heart damage, but so far, the kid was doing okay. Well, not exactly okay, but there was nothing wrong with his heart.

Whenever I see one of the boys who survived the strike, I always wonder how much it changed them. Not just the event, but the lightning itself; the electricity surging through their bodies. I don't expect they gained superpowers or anything, but were they changed somehow? Did their cosmic selection cause them to think or feel differently than before?

Could they feel a storm coming on? Or detect electrical impulses? The only thing I do know is that Brett and his dreamy eyes went on to graduate high school with a perfect GPA, garner a scholarship to the University of Tennessee, and is playing soccer for them now. Carson? Well, his life went the other direction. He started drinking heavily after the strike and began leaning heavily on his prescriptions of pain pills. Most people overlooked it because of what he'd been through and the pain his hand had to be causing him. According to the article in the paper, his life slipped slowly into darkness and he shot himself on the same soccer field where the lightning had struck him, in the same spot he was standing when it happened.

His funeral was today. Less people showed up for him than they did Avery Wheeler. A lot less. *That* was the saddest thing I've ever seen. He'd been killed by the lightning as much as Avery had. As I sat in the church looking at Brett,

I wondered what he was feeling. He, Carson, and Avery were forever connected. An unimaginable energy from the universe had seen to that, and now two of the three were dead.

I looked at him, sitting halfway back in the church in his black suit, and wondered how often he thought about what happened. Was there some existential pressure being applied to his life? Did the universe pick him for some higher calling or was he simply unlucky? Or was he the lucky one? Did he feel the need to live life to the fullest? Take advantage of the second chance? Was he worried about disappointing the universe?

I wondered a lot of things as I watched the young man who hadn't asked for any of this, but mostly I wondered if he counted himself lucky, or if he knew deep down that he would be next?

Perchance's Dream

Perchance crawled to the top of the frozen hill and peered over the crest. A cold wind swept up from the valley into his face as his eyes fell on the hulking giant in the distance. He shook his head, both glad to have found it, and not at the same time. Although over a mile away, the giant dominated the landscape in the small, flat valley. Standing over fifty feet tall, the robot had an arm span of about twenty feet, at the end of which were two vice-like metal hands. Even standing still, it was an imposing figure.

He'd seen many of them before but seeing a new one always left him with a sense of wonder. The machines were built to generally resemble a man to humanize them, but it didn't work. The giant before him stood on two rusted legs, frozen in time as it towered over the tiny huts that littered the ground around it like crumbs from some unseen cookie. He thought briefly about counting the brown thatch roofs but decided not to. It didn't really matter. There were only three sizes. The village was either big, medium, or small. This one was big.

He produced a battered pair of binoculars and pressed them to his eyes. The feet of the iron giant were rusted badly, and the left leg had holes in the steel covering it. The tops of the shoulders were rusted as well, sending dark reddish-brown streaks down the torso. Moss grew in the crevasses of the sheets of metal that covered its upper chest, living in the perpetual shadow of the oval-shaped head that was cocked slightly to one side. He trained the glasses on the giant's face and breathed a sigh of relief.

This one's eyes were closed. It didn't make a difference either way because the machines had long since fallen dormant, but seeing those wide, staring glass eyes was always a little unnerving. The sight of one of the giants alone was awe-inspiring for most people, but not him. He hated them all. He'd heard rumors throughout the years about people who'd never even seen one. It didn't sound possible, but there were rumors.

The hulks were remnants of a failed attempt by the Provisional Government, to police the people who refused to comply with the new world they found themselves living in after the Great Wars. Named Peacekeepers, the giants patrolled predetermined areas and struck fear in the hearts of men. The monstrosities obeyed only their pre-programmed orders and were heralded as a symbol of the might and intelligence of the new government. Everything was either right or wrong, allowed or not allowed. There was no gray area with the Peacekeepers.

When that government itself collapsed, the Peacekeepers were left to do what they did without upkeep or supervision. Eventually, they all fell silent, either from forces of nature or disrepair. There was talk about some that still worked, but that was doubtful. He hadn't seen one operational in forty years.

Perchance scurried back down the small rise and settled in beside his friend, Camron. He was a dark-skinned young man from somewhere far away. He was dependable and one hell of a man to have on your side in a fight. He was also the only man in the world that Perchance trusted explicitly. Despite being almost half Perchance's age, Camron had quickly risen through the ranks to become his Chief Security Officer.

"It there?" he asked, his accent making it sound like "E tear?"

Perchance nodded. "Yup. Big and rusted and ugly as hell, just like the others."

"Good. That makes it easier."

"There's a village at its feet though. Nice sized one too."

Camron pursed his lips and shook his head. "Why do they always do that?"

Perchance shrugged. "They were built to keep everyone safe. I guess they still expect it to somehow."

"A lot of bloody good those tings did," he said. "They were the work of the devil's own heart. Infernal bastards."

A slight smile came to Perchance's lips. He liked to hear his friend talk, especially when he got angry. "It's not the first time. Probably won't be the last. C'mon. Let's tell the others."

Perchance clambered down the rocky hill, careful not to lose his footing. They were running low on medical supplies and they'd need all they had when they went after the colossus. The people who worshipped it wouldn't relish the fact that they were going to destroy it. None of the others had.

Picking his way through the plain of fallen boulders, shaken from the mountainside during the wars, Perchance checked on his young friend. He was used to the cold, but Camron had grown up somewhere hot. Looking over his shoulder, he found his friend zipped tightly in his thick fur-lined coveralls with the hood cinched close over his bald head.

"You going to make it?"

"I be fine," Camron answered with a smile.

"Don't wrap up so much you start sweating. That'll make it worse."

"I be fine," Camron said again.

Perchance laughed and led them into the dense forest at the edge of the plain. Pushing his way through the underbrush, he led them back to the camp a different way than they'd left, thereby avoiding disturbing the plant life enough to be noticed by prying eyes. It was one of the many tips he'd learned at the knee of his father, an adamant survivalist.

Of course, that was all before the wars began.

The smell of cooked meat began to warm his body as he slipped into camp, unnoticed by either of the sentries he'd left on duty.

"You need to talk to your guards again," he said over his shoulder to Camron.

"I will handle it." Camron peeled off and headed toward the closest sentry post.

Perchance walked through the quiet camp, nodding to his companions as they passed. When he reached the largest of the three tents, the command tent, he pulled back the rough covering and stepped inside.

His engineer smiled at him. Although pronounced 'Rudy', he spelled his name Rooty.

"From the look on your face, I'd say you've found another one."

"You would be right too," Perchance said as he crossed the tent and drew in a long smell of the meat sizzling over the metal elements. The device, invented by Rooty, generated heat like an oven but was powered by giving the handle on the end a vigorous crank for five or six minutes. It was a time-consuming method, but it prevented them from having to make a fire to cook food. Fires made smoke and smoke signaled others that they were in the area. He'd found out a long time ago that surprise was their best tactic.

"Smells good. Deer?" Perchance asked, slipping out of his heavy coat.

"Yes. Harwell got a big male with his bow. He's turning out to be a hell of a shot with that thing."

"Good," Perchance said, nodding. They always used primitive means when hunting. Like smoke, a gunshot would travel a long way. "There's a big village at the feet of this one. About half a mile around it in every direction. The valley is fairly open after the rock plain."

Rooty nodded but continued to work on the disassembled radio on his lap. "Like up north?"

"More like that one out west. Oklahoma, I think they called it. We'll have to move in before dawn and be in a position to move at first light."

Rooty stopped working and stared at his friend for a long time before sighing and returning to his task.

"I know," Perchance replied. "That one went badly, hopefully, this won't go that way."

"I didn't say nothing."

"You don't have to. I've been thinking the same thing since I saw it." Perchance scratched the growth of gray hair on his face, his mind still on the raid Rooty's sigh was eluding to. It was by far the bloodiest battle they'd had to date. By the time they got away, eighteen members of their group and hundreds of villagers lay dead on the vast plain surrounding the Oklahoma Peacekeeper.

"I don't suppose we could talk to these people?"

"Have any of them ever listened? It's their damned god by now. You know how the villagers are." Perchance got up and went back to the makeshift cooker. "Have the others eaten?"

"All they wanted, over an hour ago. This is ours." Rooty touched a wire with the screwdriver in his hand, jumping as a blue flash arced from the wiring. "Dammit."

"There's probably no hope for that one, my friend. It took a far drop."

"Maybe I'll try later." He sat the broken radio aside and stood. "Where's Cam?"

"He's checking on the guards. We slipped right past them." Perchance picked up the butcher's knife and sliced a chunk of meat off the shank, wrapping it on a piece of flatbread.

"I suppose you've got a plan?"

Perchance nodded as he chewed his food but said nothing.

Rooty sliced his meat off and ate it off the blade, casting a wary eye at his leader. "You know, we don't have to do this."

Perchance stopped chewing and looked at his engineer, his pale green eyes burrowing into him.

Rooty wanted to shrink away, but he didn't. All leaders needed men who would question them from time to time if only to make sure they still held the beliefs they espoused. Time had a way of softening things for some men, but not Perchance.

In his leader's look, he saw the pain wrought by the "Peacekeepers". He saw his home being crushed under an iron fist. He saw his village being wiped out. He saw his mother pushing him toward the escape tunnel seconds before being killed. In his leader's look, he heard the echoes of the footfalls of a giant chasing an eleven-year-old boy. Rooty knew his leader's story well, but in his stare, he relived every terrifying moment.

"Okay," Rooty finally relented. "You know I just have to give you the option."

"There are no 'options'." The word came from his lips like it tasted bad.

Rooty looked at his leader, knowing that on the day he died, leaving one peacekeeper standing would be his biggest regret. He doubted if the man's very soul would rest until they were gone from the Earth. Perchance's story was wrought with pain and suffering, anger, and strife. Born on the day that the wars started, his very name was given to him by a mother that hoped he would be the difference in a dying civilization. She'd not only placed on him the name of hope but also written his fate when she said, "If perchance the world should crumble, let you be the last warrior standing."

No, Rooty thought. For you, there are no options, my friend.

"Tit will be a cold night."

Both men looked at Camron as he entered the tent.

"What?" he asked, looking from one to the other. "What I miss?"

"Nothing." Rooty tossed the meat into his mouth and stabbed the knife back into the meat, sending a stream of juices onto the red-hot element beneath it. "Eat up. Warm yourself, my friend. We've got plans to make."

"So it's settled then." Perchance stood and stretched his back, his eyes still on the crude drawing on the table before him. "We will rest here tomorrow and when the night comes, we will get into position. Hopefully, it will be a quick strike and we won't lose anybody. The left leg below the knee looks severely weakened by rust and decay. We will use the right leg to climb it."

"The people haven't taken very good care of their god, have they?" Camron asked as a wide smile broke out across his face.

"Be that as it may, they will still fight to keep it. Never doubt that."

"If they fight us, they will die." Perchance walked over to the heating element and gave it a few turns, warming his hands as the element began to turn red again.

"The valley floor may be muddy. It has rained recently."

"The valley floor will be frozen, and you know it, Rooty." Perchance didn't look at his engineer.

"C'mon, friends. We should be happy tonight. We have found another one of those bastards and tomorrow it will lie in ruins."

"And then what?" Rooty asked.

"Then we move on and find another one," Camron said, still smiling.

207

"And another, and another. To what end?"

"To the end of them," Perchance answered. "Until they have all been destroyed and there is no chance of anyone ever reviving them or even the idea of them. Until the grass grows green over their rusted faces and the world realizes what a mistake they were."

Rooty sighed and exchanged a glance with Camron, before dropping his gaze to his feet. "Maybe I'm getting old, maybe I'm just tired. I'll be fifty in the spring. All of this is beginning to feel futile. We're never going to change the world."

Perchance closed his eyes, struggling to contain his anger. He wasn't angry at his engineer. He wasn't angry at himself. He was angry at the Provisional Government who created the Peacekeepers. He was angry at the world they helped create. He felt dearly for the men and women in his small tribe of warriors, but he hated the Peacekeepers more.

"I'm going to check the perimeter."

Camron watched Perchance slip from the tent and then looked at Rooty. "Why do you instigate him?"

"Everyone needs to hear the voice of reason every now and then."

"The voice of reason?" Camron asked, slicing himself off a chunk of the venison. "The voice of reason died a long time ago, I'd say. About the time they decided to launch the first missiles before we were born."

"Just because I never saw those bastards in operation doesn't mean I don't know what a mess up they were."

"Mess up? That is putting it lightly. If you ever heard one walking or saw them push through a forest, you'd feel like he does."

"They're dead. Lightning killed a lot of them. The others couldn't be maintained and simply died themselves. They might as well be a tree now."

Camron shook his head. "They are not trees, my friend. Trees do not kill people. Trees do not chase people into the sea and watch them drown. People don't kill to protect the trees. Whether they're working or not, those things will never be trees. Trees are part of the natural world. Those things are not."

When the first vestiges of daylight silhouetted the hulking figure of the giant against the eastern sky, Perchance said a silent prayer for the men and women in his charge. Some of them probably wouldn't make it out of the village alive, but when the sun set, the world would be rid of one more Peacekeeper.

Lying flat on the frozen ground, his breath floating before him in plumes of smoke, Perchance looked to his left and saw Camron. His security chief looked at him and nodded. To his right, he saw Rooty. His engineer didn't look at him. His eyes were fixed on the behemoth that rose from the village a hundred yards ahead of them

Perchance closed his eyes and sighed, then got up into a crouching position. Looking back, he watched the seventy-three members of his troop do the same, almost in unison. They would all follow him into battle. He just hoped they'd all follow him out. They'd never felled a giant before without losing at least a few, but there was always hope.

He moved forward quickly, the rifle gripped in his right hand, a pair of climbers hanging around his neck. The plan was simple but effective. When they reached the giant, the thirty soldiers with climbers would assemble on one of the legs while the other formed a defense line. The first man would place his set of climbers, flat powerful magnets six inches across that were outfitted with a metal spike sticking out from the center, then move out of the way. Then the next man, then the next. The fourth man would climb the spikes set by the previous men and place his, then jump down. This would continue until they passed the knee of the giant. Now too far to jump safely, the sixth man would stay, and magnets would be passed up the chain. He would climb higher with each set of magnets until he reached the waist of the Peacekeeper. There, explosives would be attached and the fuse lit.

The sixth man assumed most of the risk because he was completely dependent upon the troop to keep the villagers away. High above the fray, the sixth man would be visible and an easy target. Today, just like every time before, Perchance was the sixth man.

Circling the village, they approached from the south and slipped between the crude huts ringing the settlement. Moving in unison, they all spread out and made their way around darkened huts, moving quietly, but quickly. Although the conditions made it difficult for them, cold winter mornings were the best times to attack. The simple villagers would be comfortably tucked in their beds, reluctant to rise early and face the bitter cold.

Perchance smiled, happy with their advancement. Maybe, he thought, maybe today we won't lose anyone. The hope was still on his lips when the sound of a horn pierced the darkness.

The troop abandoned their attempts at stealth and rushed forward, amassing at the right foot of the giant. As the first shots rang out, Perchance heard the first set of climbers strike the cold steel of the giant with a solid, *thunk, thunk*. He began returning fire as the troop began to build the ladder behind him, dropping two villagers as they exited their huts. He slung his rifle over his shoulder and moved into position as the troop moved with trained precision. Finally, it was his turn.

The coldness of the steel bit into his bare hand as he raced up the spikes, applied his climbers, then climbed higher. He accepted another set of magnets and placed them, then another set. A bullet ricocheted off the steel above his head and he laughed. They wouldn't hit him. He believed it with every ounce of his being. He was doing noble work and would be protected by all the ancient gods.

When he finally secured the last of the climbers to the waist of the giant, he affixed a short rope tied around his waist to it. His frozen hands went inside the thick coat and produced two heavy, gray bricks. He pressed them against the cold steel and poked a fuse into the lump as another bullet sang past his ear.

He took out a Zippo lighter, cupping one hand around it to shield it from the icy wind, and lit the fuse. Unleashing himself from the giant, he began working his way down the spikes. Using a long knife, its blade made of aluminum, he pried each set of climbers loose and dropped them to waiting arms below.

Halfway down the leg, a bullet struck the steel of the machine and ricocheted past his face, grazing his cheek. He ran a hand over his face and looked at the dark streaks of blood on his fingers before continuing his feverish work. The safe time was ninety-two seconds. Anything past that would put them in the blast zone.

The count running in his mind told him that thirty seconds had passed already.

He stabbed the knife between the steel and another magnet and ripped it free with a grunt. As he turned to drop the set, a searing pain roared through his shoulder. He knew what it was immediately. He'd been shot before.

He clenched his teeth against the pain and worked one-handed to remove the rest of the magnets before jumping off the fourth spike. As his feet landed on the cold ground, the smell of smoke and gunpowder filled his nose, and another shot struck him in the side.

He passed the knife off to Camron and unslung his rifle, firing several shots in rapid succession. The villagers were pushing in close. "Let's go!" he screamed. "We're at forty seconds."

The group surrounded their wounded leader and began fighting their way out of the village through an angry mob filled with righteous indignation. The villagers knew who they were and what they were here to do and were fighting to save their god.

The troop, now down several guns, was still in the village when the deafening roar of the explosion rolled across the valley. The villagers stopped fighting and stared up at the fireball.

Camron took Perchance's arm and slung it over his shoulder. "Let's go," he screamed as the sound of screeching metal filled the air.

The villagers rushed to the center of town just in time to watch their giant lurch to one side, teeter for a second, then fall to the ground with a crash, flattening several of the nearby huts. The people stood silent in their rags with their mouths agape as they stared in disbelief. A woman in the crowd began to wail loudly as she pushed through the stunned crowd. She went to the fallen giant and dropped to her knees beside it, crying.

"Who would do such a thing?" one man asked, joining the woman. "Why? Why?"

"Oh great Peacekeeper, forgive us for our failures. Forgive us for not protecting you," the woman cried. "Forgive our egregious sin."

"The raiders!" a man shouted. "The raiders did this to us!"

"What will we do now?" someone whined.

The crowd began to call for the heads of the raiders, chanting for their deaths.

"Who will go after them?" one man asked, standing before the crowd. "They've escaped the village. Who will bring them back?" He surveyed the crowd as the chants began to fade. "Look what they have done." He stretched one hand toward the twisted remnants of the giant's legs and the other toward the broken shell of its body. "Will no one avenge the destruction of our great Peacekeeper?"

"But they're in the yellow zone by now, and soon to be in the red. We cannot go out there."

The man looked at the crowd and shook his head. "But what are we to do now?" he asked before staggering away, his head hanging low.

"They're not chasing us," Camron said, grinning as he lugged Perchance across the valley floor.

"Good. That's good," Perchance whispered, his free hand pressed to his side to stem the flow of blood.

"You going to be okay."

"I don't know. It hurts like hell and I'm losing a lot of blood." Perchance raised his bloody hand before him as he staggered alongside his friend. He shook his head and put his hand back over the wound.

"We get you back to camp, you be fine."

"Slow down. There's no hurry. Tell the others to go ahead so we can talk."

"No. No. Don't start that shit with me, Perchance."

Perchance smiled at his friend. "Please."

A wave of sadness washed over Camron's face as tears welled in his eyes. "Go ahead, get back to camp," he yelled to the group, waving them past him. "We will be along shortly."

He forced an excited cheer as they streamed past. When the last of the group had gone ahead, leaving Camron and Perchance alone, they slowed to a walk.

"You know, when I first saw you, I thought you were an idiot."

Camron laughed. "This is what you want to tell me?"

"No," Perchance said, a smile tugging at the corners of his mouth. "But when I got to know you, I realized you were a good man. A better man than me."

"Maybe you were the idiot."

"Look, Cam, you've been with me for a long time. I'm not afraid to say we couldn't have done what we've done without you. You've been a good soldier, a good man, and a better friend."

"Well," Camron said, adjusting Perchance's arm around his neck. "Was either be with you or be in a village like that one. I do not like to be afraid all the time."

"Do you know why I started all this?"

"You do not like robots?"

Perchance laughed, then grimaced. "That is true."

Camron looked at his friend. His breath was coming in short, labored pants. He didn't have much longer and he wanted to say something.

"My dad was a great man. He never was in any type of official position, but he was a great leader. Other men looked to him for answers. I remembered seeing them come to the house and talk to him. When the blasts happened, he helped people get things back together. Everything was in chaos all around us, but in our little house things were right as rain."

Perchance coughed and stopped walking, casting his eyes to the boulder plain ahead of them. "My mother said he was a rock. When things changed, he stayed the same. He weathered the lightning storms without a complaint. He hunted and fished and grew our food and gave away plenty. He protected us from raiders countless times, and other people's houses as well. For all my life he never changed. He just adapted to whatever situation he was in."

"He sounds like a great father."

"He was." Perchance motioned for Camron to let him sit down against one of the larger boulders that had rolled into the plain and he complied. He settled on the cold ground and leaned against the stone with a pained grunt.

"But as great as he was, my mom was greater. She never spoke ill of anyone. When my father went to fight in the wars, it was just us two. I took over for my father and tried to be great as he was. Before long, people were coming to me for advice. Imagine that. A nine, ten-year-old kid. My mother said it was because they needed to believe in something, in someone."

Camron watched Perchance cough and took off his thick overcoat, draping it over his legs as he knelt on the frozen ground next to his friend.

"When my father came back from the wars, he was different. He was afraid. I never saw him afraid before, but he was then. He didn't act like it, but I could see it in his eyes. We did find that winter, but in the spring the Peacekeeper that patrolled our area started getting closer and closer. I asked my father what we should do. He said we should hide. That's when we started digging the escape tunnels."

"That makes sense to me."

"One day a bunch of us guys decided to go and fight the Peacekeeper. We built this trap." Perchance grimaced and pressed his hand to his side.

"You've told me this story."

"Not all of it." Perchance doubled over as pain wracked his body. When the pain eased, he sat back up. "We went out and found it, but it killed three of us straight away. Like that." He snapped his fingers weakly before letting his hand drop back to his lap. "It was horrible hearing them scream, but I knew we were in for it then, so I fought on. We ended up breaking its eyes out and then tricked it into walking off a cliff. We all cheered when that son of a bitch smashed itself to bits on the rocks. We laughed and cheered. When my father found out, he was mad as hell. He spanked me and called me selfish."

Perchance looked up at the morning sky and shook his head, a sad smile on his lips. "Within a month there was another Peacekeeper. He climbed the mountain and came straight for our little village. It came for us because I fought and killed the other one. I brought it to us, and it killed everybody in the village except me."

"That's not your fault, man. You were a child."

"My mother never blamed me like my father did. She said I was just trying to find out what being a leader was. Once, late one night, she said she was proud of me for killing the peacekeeper. She said she wished they were all dead. That they were evil machines."

"She was right, too."

Perchance shrugged. "I guess she was. The night it came to our village she was reading the old bible to me. I don't know which one. But there was this story about this kid who killed a giant with a rock and a sling." He wiped a tear from the corner of his eye. "I said, 'that's like me', and she smiled. I'll never forget it. She said I was a giant slayer. That was what I was born to be."

"Aye, and you're the best."

"Do you know what my name means?"

Camron shook his head. "I just thought you had a funny name."

Perchance smiled. "It means 'if by some chance'. She said that's why she named me that. She always said, if by some chance this world gets any better, it will be because of men like you."

Camron inhaled deeply, struggling to maintain his composure. He looked back toward the eastern sky where the giant once stood. The soft rays of the morning sun lit the valley, now free of the hulking mechanism that dominated the landscape for the last fifty years. A thin trail of smoke rose from the village, marking the spot of their latest victim.

"The valley definitely looks better without dat thing," he said. As he turned back to Perchance, his smile faded. He looked at his friend's still, lifeless body and began to cry. He leaned forward and pulled Perchance's body in a tight embrace, weeping openly as a cold wind ripped across the valley.

Camron held his friend close for a long time before finally laying him on the ground. He stood and looked around, surveying the valley. "Someday," he said as the wind gusted in his face, "this place will hold evidence of the death of a great man."

Camron scratched the patchy gray hair on his face as he approached the podium, a man half his age holding his elbow. He laid the speech that he'd only helped write down and cleared his throat, causing the microphone before him to squeal with feedback. The same younger man came forward and adjusted it in front of him.

The old man stood on tired legs and looked out over the throngs of people before him. Stretching as far as his failing eyes could see, they stood in the warm sunshine and waited for him to speak. He looked out over the valley, seeing it for only the second time in his life. His eyes went to the towering figure before him, draped in a massive tarp, and he smiled.

"Today," he began, then cleared his throat. "Today is the realization of the dream of many, many people that you've never met. Great people, strong people who dared to hope in the face of hopelessness. People who dared to fight in the face of fear. People who dared to dream in the darkest of nights. That dream survived the great blasts, suffered through the lightning storms, fought in the Great Wars, and suffered beneath the feet of mechanical beasts. The dream that you enjoy today began as a dream of a woman who dared to hope for a better future and named her son Perchance."

Camron paused when a great cheer went up. He smiled as he thumbed a tear from his cheek. His friend had grown into a legend these last sixty years.

"Perchance once told me that in an old text that his mother read to him, there was a tale of a young boy who was brave enough to fight a giant," he paused, smiling as another cheer went up from the crowd. "Ruth Davis told her son, only moments before she was killed by a peacekeeper, that if this world was going to get any better it would be because of brave men like him." He wiped another tear while waiting for the raucous crowd to settle down.

"I know that there were many men and women who fought the Peacekeepers, who strove to get us to where we are today, but every army needs a general, every movement needs a leader, every hope needs shoulders to ride on, and those shoulders belonged to my dear, dear friend, Perchance. He gave his life to help build the world we now enjoy. We've still got a long way to go, but because of men like him, we have the chance to get there."

Camron extended his hands to the figure before him. A deafening roar filled the air as the tarp began to fall, revealing the statue of Perchance. Standing with a rifle in his hand and a pair of binoculars to his face, it looked out over the plain, ever searching for the next Peacekeeper while one foot rested on the ruins of a dead giant.

The aid stepped forward and waved his hands to quieten the crowd. When they calmed down, Camron leaned closer to the microphone.

"My friend wasn't big on speeches and neither am I. I just want to leave you with this, and I hope you carry it with you everywhere you go." Camron drew in a deep breath and blew it out slowly.

"If, perchance, the day comes when the world needs a hero, let that hero be found in all of us."

The crowd erupted into applause as a hand slipped gently around his waist. Turning, he put his arms around the young woman and hugged her to him.

"You did good, daddy. You ready to go home now?"

Camron looked at his daughter, smiling as he cradled her cheek in his hand, then stared at the statue of his friend for a long time. When he turned back to his daughter tears were streaming down his face.

"Yeah, baby." He answered with a weak nod but didn't move.

The young woman followed his gaze to the statue of a man she never met. She rubbed his back lovingly as they stared at it in silence. The sadness on his face broke her heart.

"You miss him, don't you?"

"I do," he nodded. "To the world, he was a hero, but to me, he was my friend. That's what I miss the most."

The Opening of a Grave

Southerners are a peculiar people. I can attest to this because I am one, and I too am peculiar at times. Nothing, however, brings out these peculiarities as much as births and deaths. Births are wonderful, joyous occasions. Even when the parents are young and stupid and "don't have a pot to piss in or a window to throw it out of", we celebrate the beginning of a new life and the promises it holds. The smell of that lotion they put on babies' heads might also have something to do with it too, I'm not sure, but births are big.

Deaths, on the other hand, bring on a whole onslaught of conflicting emotions for everyone involved. People grieve, or rather show their grief in about as many ways as there is to die. Some people love attending funerals, some don't. Some people show their emotions, some don't. Lots of people bring food to the bereaved families, and lots of food gets tossed because that same bereaved family knows the woman who cooked it doesn't keep a clean house and wouldn't be caught dead eating her food. "They got three cats in the house" is a perfectly legitimate reason to toss a whole casserole without even unwrapping it.

Like I said, we're a peculiar people.

Still, in my thirties, I hadn't given a great deal of thought to the subject of death even though it had visited my door a couple of times. That all changed when a wife of a dear friend of mine called one summer morning. My friend's wife explained to my wife that her husband's mother had died and that he was hellbent to dig her grave himself.

It was a hot, muggy day in mid-August in the deep south. The humidity was marching towards 90 percent and the temperature was outpacing it. There wasn't a cloud in the sky and the weatherman was already issuing warnings about the heat. This was definitely not a day to be doing hard physical labor out in the sun.

When she asked if I would help her husband, naturally I agreed even though I had no idea what the request entailed. My mind conjured up images of old men in heavy, black coats skulking around a cemetery in the middle of the night, always a little dirty and usually with the smell of cheap liquor on their breath. Putting aside what I had planned to do that day, which was as little as possible, I grabbed a bottle of water and headed out.

I'd never been to the church but had a general idea where it was. The bumpy dirt road it was on ambled along through a huge swath of reclaimed forest. After being logged many years ago, the land was replanted with pines that had grown almost big enough to be cut again. The bright morning sun shone through the pine tops at regular intervals, casting long shadows across the road. The result was an alternating, sun, shade pattern that messed with your eyes if you drove fast enough. Fortunately, I wasn't in a big hurry.

I emerged from the forest at the edge of a fair-sized graveyard that led up to a rather small country church. I pulled off in a shady spot on the opposite side of the road of the cemetery and got out, looking at the row of tombstones whose years on this earth easily surpassed mine.

He stopped digging, already sweating profusely, and looked at me as I approached. "What're you doing here?" he asked breathlessly.

"Just passing through and saw you. Thought you might need a hand," I lied.

Shrugging, he went back to work. He was a man of few words. It was as much an invitation as I was going to get.

I surveyed the damage done to the dry, brown grass with dismay, hoping for more progress. A rectangular frame of rusty metal about an inch wide had been traced on the ground with blue spray paint before being cast aside. It now lay haphazardly against Emma Parker's tombstone, whoever she was. Most of the edges of the blue rectangle had been assaulted with a shovel, removing large chunks of the red clay and the Bahia grass that grew in it, neither of which looked too happy to be disturbed.

I grabbed a pickaxe and decided to work on the center of the rectangle. Raising the pick high above my head, I brought it hurtling earthward with a mighty groan. The rusted metal dove through the hot, still air and slammed into the gravesite with a dull thud that resonated through the worn, wooden handle and into my hands. It penetrated to a depth of about two inches before coming to an abrupt stop. I rubbed my hands together to relieve the tingling then pried it loose and looked at it, disappointed. My herculean effort yielded a small divot in the unforgiving dirt.

"It's pretty compacted," he said. I agreed and hefted the pick again, and again, and again. Each time I struck the earth with as much force as I could muster, and each time it penetrated the same two inches. It was going to be a long day.

He suggested spelling me and I gave only a weak argument while handing over the pick. He, being considerably larger and more adept at such things as digging graves, managed a three-inch penetration, each swing prying chunks of hard, red clay from the site.

"Gonna be here a while," he panted when he finally took a break long enough to wipe the sweat from his eyes.

"I got all day," I told him, and I did. I just hadn't planned on working this hard on my day off. As he went back to picking at the compacted earth, I spared a moment to look across the graveyard. The old, weathered tombstones testified to its age. This was an old country church and a lot of old country people had been laid to rest here, undoubtedly while people sang "Amazing Grace" or "May the Circle Be Unbroken" and the preacher said a few words, some of which might have applied to the poor souls being laid to rest.

By this point in my life, I had already been to several funerals and most of them were in country churches. My grandparents on my mother's side and my mother herself were currently residing in the ground outside a church even more remote than this one. Until that day I never considered who had dug their graves, but I gained a sincere appreciation for them.

Working with the shovel, I dug chunks of ground out of the shallow indentation and tossed them onto the rapidly growing pile next to us, amazed at the fact that the pile of dirt looked to be twice the amount of what came out of the hole. I made note of this to my friend and quickly learned that once free of its earthly confines, dirt expands and loosens itself.

Mildly amused and pleased to have learned something that I didn't know that I didn't know, I went back to work beneath the merciless sun. Together, we got the hole about a foot deep and stopped for water. I had a bottle in my truck seat, and he had one sitting in the shade of a tombstone dedicated to Joshua Parker, no doubt kin to old Emma. He suggested we take our refreshments to the shade and I agreed.

We sat in silence and watched the air dance over the cemetery. The heat reflected off the ground and rose through the air in a shimmering wave, making the trees on the far side look as if they were moving. It always reminded me of that illusion one creates by holding a pencil loosely on one end moving up and down quickly. When done properly, the pencil looks like it's made of rubber, bending as it moved up and down in an undulating wave.

I drank half my lukewarm water and looked at him. "Sorry to hear about your mama."

"Thanks," was all he said. I didn't figure he wanted to talk about it. I'd gone through the same thing about ten years earlier and I never did want to talk about it. There wasn't much to say that would make a difference anyway. I was overseas with the Navy and didn't get back until the night before her funeral. We buried her and I spent the rest of my leave drinking heavily.

"No problem."

Leaving the rest of our refreshments for later, when they'd be even warmer, we marched unenthusiastically back across the dirt road and into the cemetery. Deciding on a different approach, we both took up pickaxes. He positioned himself at the head of the plot, according to the layout of all the other graves, and I took up the foot end. Taking turns, we each took a swing at the dirt in the grave, loosening it chunk by chunk until we'd finished a three-inch layer.

It was a triumph of teamwork and precision, not unlike the workers of old pounding in spikes on the trans-continental railroad track. One man would swing then retract his tool, then the other. Back and forth, one catching his breath while the other assaulted the earth, keeping it under constant attack. There was a rhythm to the pain that lent itself to song, maybe something about John Henry, or "Sweet Chariot," but we didn't sing. It was too damned hot to sing.

Using this strategy, we pounded the hole to a depth of three feet before the molten orb of lava in the sky forced us back into the shade for a brief respite. We crawled out of the hole with tired muscles and sweat-soaked shirts. The sun, right above us now, beat us like a man holding a grudge, pushing the temperature somewhere between a furnace and a welding torch, and the humidity was determined not to be outdone.

Having finished our water, we made small talk in the shade-which only lowered the temperature a few degrees–unwilling to reenter the theatre in which we were doing battle. We were halfway through, and three quarters wore down. It was going to be close.

Unlike the Wild West days–when someone could take a shovel and dig through loose, sandy soil and bury a person without messing up the bandana around his neck, then still have the energy to court a beautiful, young woman–digging a grave was very specific. Way more so than I'd thought it would be, not that I ever really thought about.

For instance, the rectangular frame wasn't just a way to plot out the site. The entire structure had to fit in the grave and slide down the walls to a depth of six feet. The walls had to be straight, square, and more or less smooth. This was accomplished by a specific set of tools intended for just such work: grave tools. It wasn't a fancy name, but they didn't do fancy work. The shovels, both rounded and flat-edged, and picks were pretty common, but there is also something called a straight hoe. It was a tool that looked like a regular garden hoe but without the curved neck. It was intended to be used from ground level to chop and shave the walls. A short hoe, which was pretty much a regular hoe, but with a short, thick handle and a more substantial head. It too was used to smooth and shape the walls, but from inside the pit.

I also learned that there were even names for digging and filling in the hole. First, you opened the grave, then after the funeral, the grave was closed. Turns out that even in death there were certain technicalities and legal responsibilities that had to be fulfilled, like the depth, breadth, and length of a hole. Even if a really short person was to be buried, the hole still had to be a precise size to accommodate a vault. The concrete form lowered into the grave wasn't technically required, but almost everyone had one. Then the sealed casket would be placed inside the vault and a concrete lid would be laid atop it. Not many people saw this because all the real work was done before and after the short amount of time spent by friends and family at the graveside services.

We'd made it to five feet when his wife showed up with drinks and snacks. To us, she was no less noble than a Red Cross disaster relief crew. We were nearly spent, out of water, and neither of us had had much to eat. I do believe if she hadn't shown up, they might have found two bodies already occupying the grave when they went to lower his mama into it.

The cold drinks and peanut butter crackers were manna from heaven, which we chomped down like a couple of hungry wolves. Afterward, we sat in the shade of a towering white oak, our clothes stained with red dirt, and watched the sun bake the recently unearthed mound next to the grave. I

229

wiped a bead of sweat away as it ran down the side of my face and sighed. As undesirable as it was, we both knew we had to get back out in the sun. Like a boxer who was taking a beating, but determined to finish the fight, we stood with achy, reluctant groans. Kissing his wife goodbye –him, not me– we went back to work and removed the last foot of red clay from the bottom of the pit.

Standing at the bottom of a freshly dug grave gives you a strange perspective. Six feet in the ground feels deeper than it sounds, especially when you're just under six feet tall. The striations and colors of the different layers of dirt revealed in the cross-section of earth looked almost like art to me. Staring at the earth within its walls recounted the history of the land in ways that are rarely considered. It was a pleasant respite from the task at hand, if only momentarily.

I wondered on which layer had the pioneers trod. What dirt was under the feet of the Native Americans who once populated this area? Was one of the stripes of colored dirt the effect of an ancient volcano? Or maybe a great flood? My mind was reeling with questions.

When he offered a hand, I took it and he helped haul me from the grave, then jumped in himself. His muddy boots struck the bottom with a hollow thump. After four failed tries, during which we would have to shave more dirt from the wall in the places where the frame snagged, I handed the frame over the edge praying that it would fit. When it slid to the bottom, he let out a thankful grunt and handed it back to me. As unenthusiastic as it was, it did say that we were done.

It was finally over. We'd dug a grave. The profoundness of such a monumental task seemed lost on my friend, perhaps because it was a grave for his mother, not mine. The whole situation probably felt completely different to him.

I looked at the mountain of dirt next to us, then at the hole that it had come from, and shook my head in disbelief. The pile of loose dirt was twice the size of the hole it had been evicted from. The tape measure said we'd dug a neat, six-foot by four-foot hole straight down to the depth of six feet one inch. We were hot, sweaty, dirty, and tired but most importantly, we were done.

When I came back with a bottle of water he was sitting on the edge of the grave, looking at the bottom through his muddy work boots. I nudged him with the bottle and offered it to him. He drank half of it thirstily before pouring the rest over his head.

There was no doubt in my mind that he was thinking about his mother laying in her casket in the hole we'd wrought from the compacted, uncooperative earth, and maybe pondering the finality of death and the preciousness of life. I had never met his mother, but I did help dig her grave. I didn't dig it for her. I dug it for my friend.

For me it was a novelty, digging a grave, but for him, it must have been cathartic in some way; a fulfillment of some final duty, the reparation for some wrong, or maybe it just needed to be done and no one else would do it. Maybe it was simply one last act that a man could do for his mother. Either way we had moved one hundred forty-four cubic feet of begrudging Alabama dirt from the ground on what I would learn later was one of the hottest days of the year and we had survived, that was something to be proud of.

I clapped him on the shoulder as he sat on the edge of his mother's grave and said, "Love ya, brother." I turned and walked toward my truck. I stopped at the edge of the dusty road and looked back at him, framed against the backdrop of the mound of dirt, and my heart ached for him. "If you need help with the closing let me know."

He threw a hand up but never replied. He didn't have to. I know he appreciated the help and the company. I got into my truck and turned it back down the gravel lane. Glancing in the rearview mirror a few times as I rode away, I saw him sitting where I'd left him. He was still there when I rounded a curve and headed for home.

The birth of a novel:

My latest novel began life as the short story you are about to read. The short story started from a writing prompt I saw. The picture was of a man dressed in surgical scrubs, his eyes bandaged with dirty gauze, wandering through a desert. The sense of helplessness that the man must have felt struck a chord with me. It was a very powerful picture. I never pursued the writing prompt contest, but I did write the story. My nephew liked the story and urged me to write more. Thinking that it wouldn't be enough for a novel, I thought about publishing it as a series of short stories on my website. After I wrote the second and third short stories, the plot began to develop itself and I thought I might have something.

The thing with the way I write is that I'm dependent on the characters to speak to me, to take control of their own lives, and to make their own decisions. I know it sounds crazy, but that's just what they do in my mind. If I try to steer them, things just don't flow. I can write them to do what I want, but it doesn't feel right. For better or worse, I allow the story to develop on its own.

This story was extremely challenging in that the main character is blind, and a genius- neither of which applies to me. It was hard to not use visual indicators at all. No "He looked at her", or "She was beautiful in the morning light." It posed a unique situation, to say the least. Another thing that I did set out to intentionally do which appears later in the novel is that the female lead character, a Yemeni woman whose first language is not English, doesn't use contractions when she speaks English. It may sound simple, but as a writer, writing dialogue without any contractions is quite odd.

In the end, I had a novel full of action, set in the middle of a desert, where two completely different people must come together and survive in one of the most inhospitable places on Earth while thwarting Facility agents, escaping gun runners, and avoiding the U.S. military who is eager to remove an American citizen with a growing list of bodies in his wake before he lands in the middle of an international incident.

The Man with No Eyes will be released in 2021 by Gnat Smoke Press and will be available on all major markets in e-book and print format as well as Barnes & Noble and other retailers.

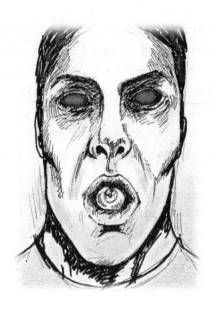

The Man with no Eyes

It's like drowning only worse, Andrew thought as the heat pressed against his face, washing over him in one continuous scorching wave. It took a conscious effort not to fixate on it, but it was impossible to ignore.

It was everywhere. It hung on the dry air and rose from the loose sand that crunched underfoot. It pressed in from every direction, surrounding his body with an almost palpable force.

His mind groped for the words of an old song about the desert being an ocean or was the ocean a desert? Maybe. Or was the desert an ocean? He shook his head, momentarily considering raising his recall function, but decided against it. He needed to conserve his energy. He'd lowered all non-essential functions and devoted the energy to life support systems. The song didn't matter. What mattered was surviving the heat.

He took in a deep breath and blew it out slowly, stopping himself from obsessing over the heat, again. A part of him was glad that he couldn't see the sand stretching to the horizon in every direction. The psychological effect would be difficult to overcome. But then again, if he could see, he might not be here, to begin with.

He had further to go than he'd come, and the idea that he'd both underestimated the desert and overestimated his abilities was beginning to take hold. He'd been stumbling through the desert one night and a day and he was still no closer to freedom than when he left the Facility.

He let out an angry grunt as the name entered his mind. The Facility. The place he used to work had a long, official-sounding name, but no one ever used it. In his years there, he never heard it called anything else, even when they were courting him to join their work.

In retrospect, the subtle isolation was part of a carefully crafted plan. Even when he'd been flown in on the company helicopter, a retro-fitted Blackhawk, it had been at night. It was all to keep the exact location as secret as possible. Not that he would have noticed anyway, with all the champagne and the smoke they were blowing up his ass.

Despite coming to the same conclusion many times already, he diverted his thoughts to doing the math of his survival. Again. It was an exercise in futility because of the variables, but it was better than thinking about the heat.

Assuming a walking speed of twenty minutes per mile and a continuous pace, it would take him nearly fourteen days to reach civilization, rumored to be a thousand miles away. He had been walking almost twenty-four hours, barely seventy-five miles, but he had rested twice already. So much for the continuous pace. Each break was about an hour, so that was a minus of six miles. Nine hundred thirty-four to go, give or take the life of one man.

Of course, that was all dependent upon finding water. If that didn't happen, he would be dead, and all the math would be moot anyway.

Unless... his mind reminded him. That was what he was counting on. Unless he did find water. He had pinned his hopes on another rumor, an oasis. He'd never actually seen it, but there were a few whispers from people who were "gifted" the opportunity to visit it.

Unfortunately, there were other "unlesses" to consider. Unless he came upon a desert snake and got bitten. Or a scorpion, or a spider. Or some other godforsaken creature that lived in this hellhole. Unless he tripped and fell and broke a leg.

Unless they came after him.

If they did come after him, he wouldn't be hard to find. Footprints in the sand would be easy to follow, and a man stumbling along with his eyes wrapped in dirty gauze, wearing the blue-green scrubs of a surgeon didn't exactly blend in with the environment. He was far enough away for the Facility's chopper to find him in five minutes.

Andrew shook his head at the thought but kept walking. It would be a depressing thought for the average man, but he was not an average man. He was a special man with special abilities, which was why the Facility really wanted him to begin with.

In his old life, he was considered a genius. At the Facility, he was just another cog in the works. With an IQ that hovered around the high 160s, coupled with his abilities, he was as much a subject as he was a contributor. They paid him for his surgical prowess, but they wanted him for his abilities.

His ability to control every system of his body, down to a cellular level was a physiological anomaly. He could isolate and contain any pathogen. He could use his body's own faculties to heal himself at an accelerated rate. His mind held vast reservoirs of visual records from almost everything he'd ever seen. His memory was a vault. This ability had countless medical possibilities, making him invaluable to the scientists at the Facility.

It was also the only reason he even considered escaping.

The Facility was also a special place with special abilities, the most prevalent of which was to not get bogged down by ethics or basic human rights.

Life there was an experience in duality. If you did what they wanted the world was your oyster. You'd be fed the finest food and housed in the lap of luxury. They had the money and clout to satisfy every whim, except hard drugs. If you wanted beautiful women, you got beautiful women. If you wanted a little boy, you got a little boy. Of course, they would be locals from one of the villages within reach, but ethnicity didn't seem to matter when the dark perversions of the human mind were given free rein. When you were done, they would take care of any messes that arose.

If you didn't comply, your life would be an agonizing hell. If you didn't do what they wanted, your son would end up one of the little boys requested. If your wife were nice looking, like his was, she would end up one of the special requests. And you would watch and listen to every second of it while your coworkers lived out their twisted fantasies.

So often the thing about great minds was that great perversion and savagery lay tucked neatly in the folds of genius. Remove any societal restraint and the ugly comes to the surface quickly.

The hard truth was that the Facility had ways of getting what they wanted. The part they left out of the recruitment brochure was that working there was a lifelong commitment. How long you stayed was up to you, but their secrets had to be kept at all costs.

The head of the Facility, Alain Savon was a sadistic lunatic. The only thing he liked better than satisfying his own sexual perversions was the power that he wielded with an iron fist. Savon didn't like to be told no, and he never lost. He understood how to motivate people to do what he wanted. By sugar or by salt, he always got what he wanted. Always. Savon was a master of mind games and ruthlessly efficient in everything he did.

As far as Andrew could tell, he was the first person to tell Savon no, and he'd paid a great price for it. His foolishly noble efforts had gained him nothing and cost him his family. After being forced to watch as his wife and son were brutalized and murdered, Savon ordered that his eyes be surgically removed to ensure that the last thing he ever saw was the effects of defying his orders; as the people he loved were brutalized and murdered.

Andrew plodded along at a steady pace. His body was on autopilot since his escape, and it navigated the gently undulating sand with ease. His body temperature was elevated enough to cause a bit of perspiration to cool it, but not enough to hasten dehydration. He had diminished all other functions except his sense of smell to preserve energy.

Topping a small rise, he paused and ran a hand over his short hair. He had grown it half an inch since leaving the Facility to shield his head from the sun. It was still hot, but better than the shaved head he'd left the Facility with.

He put his sweaty palm to his mouth. The salt and moisture immediately soaked into the dryness of his tongue, igniting the cracked tissue. He grimaced as he slowly swept his face across the desert, smelling the wind.

It was blowing out of the east, represented in his mind by a series of long, neon green vector arrows. The green arrows always denoted the wind. The varying pitch and speed painted a picture of the vastness of the land before him as the arrows moved across the uneven sand. Different shades of yellow and orange represented the sound of everything else. Blue was the color of favor, and red always meant danger. His visualization techniques were still a work in process, and a far cry from the man who had taught him, but his abilities and determination were strengthening them with each passing day.

There was a faint smell in the air that was different from yesterday. Flowers? Vegetation? Water? It was hard to be sure, but something had changed.

Increasing his pace slightly, he corrected his direction and started off with the wind in his face. It was probably his last chance. Another day without water would push him into dangerous territory. Even a man with his abilities had limitations.

The first time Daniel Souter saw the doctor approaching, creeping in on his hands and knees in the twilight, he mistook him for a desert animal. The shape paused, looked around, and listened, then crept closer, repeating the process until he was at the edge of the oasis.

Souter remained motionless, waiting. When he realized the shape was a man, he smiled knowingly. The doctor had arrived.

The thin, streamlined goggles affixed to his face were set to FLIR, forward-looking infrared, allowing him his secret observation. Sitting against the trunk of a desert palm in his usual dark green military-style cargo pants and khaki shirt, he would be hard to spot even if the man coming towards him had sight.

That was his job, to be undetected and to notice things that average people missed. He was head of security at the premier medical research facility on the Arabian Peninsula and thus not very well-liked, but that was okay. In truth, he relished the fact that people disliked him. They disliked him because they feared him. It felt good to be feared instead of being afraid. Finally.

Unlike the good doctor, who was slowly making his way toward him, he was born blind and had remained so until Alain Savon had given him his sight at the age of eighteen. So many things had changed over the years, but he never forgot the gift he'd received. When a man gives you sight, you remain loyal to him no matter what.

He becomes your personal Jesus.

Souter watched the doctor make his way to the edge of the small oasis, just like he knew he would. There was nowhere else to go, they were in the middle of the desert. If the doctor was a genius like they said he was, he wasn't much of one. He'd just been outsmarted by a high school dropout.

Hiding just behind a small palm, the doctor waited and cocked his head to listen for any sign of danger. He turned his face to the source of the water and drew in a deep breath through his nose.

After another short hesitation, he scrambled into the small clearing and approached the water. Reaching down, he scooped up a palm full and tested it, waiting a full five minutes to feel the effects of it in his mouth before swallowing it.

Souter watched and waited. The doctor was disciplined, there was no denying that. He didn't have a personal issue with Doctor Harkins himself. He was just doing his job and the doctor was just another one of the arrogant men who walked around like they were better than everyone else; just another rich man who would walk past a blind kid begging on the street without even noticing.

On second thought, maybe this is personal, Souter thought as his jaw clenched tighter.

Satisfied with the water, Andrew lowered his face to the pool's surface and drank heartily before washing his face and wetting his short hair, now almost a full inch longer than when he'd left the Facility. Sitting up with a sigh of relief, his hand went out and began exploring the area. He found a large boulder near the water's edge and ran a hand along the stone. Leaning against it, he slid down onto the sand with a tired sigh.

Inside the goggles, Souter's eyes moved to the heads-up display at the edge of his field of vision and focused on the small icon of an eye in the upper right corner. The goggles transitioned from infrared to plain vision.

Looking at Andrew Harkins, Souter considered the irony of the situation. He was looking at a man with his own eyes. It had to be the first time in history that a man's eyes looked back at him while resting in another man's head, albeit aided by a pair of fancy goggles.

Instead of simply blinding the doctor for his betrayal, Savon had ordered a lengthy surgery to remove Andrew Harkin's eyes. He then had them implanted in him. It made perfect sense to not waste such a valuable commodity.

When the bandages came off everyone marveled at the miracle of the event, but all he knew was that he could finally see color.

The goggles he now wore were the realization of a dream for Alain Savon and a shining achievement for the Facility. The addition of the human eyes had improved his vision dramatically. Before, with the old goggles that Savon had attached to his face so many years ago, his vision was a field of varying shades of gray generated by the processors in the goggles. Those images were then passed to his optic nerves, allowing him to "see". It was limited sight with no real details, but for a boy who knew only darkness, it was heaven. He couldn't begin to understand the technology, but he didn't care. The results spoke for themselves.

The ability, and willingness, to do the things they did, was what made the Facility great and he was proud to be a small part of it. They were leaps and bounds ahead of anyone in biotronics, medical implantation, and human-computer integration. They were the pinnacle of success and the envy of the world. They charged top dollar for their technology and business was booming.

Souter sat motionless, barely breathing, with his finger against the trigger of the nine-millimeter on his lap. He could kill the doctor at any moment without him ever knowing who had done it. If he was intently listening, he might hear a finger gently squeeze the trigger an instant before he died, but he wasn't listening intently. He was resting.

Besides, his orders were to bring the good doctor back alive. He could still be of service to the Facility.

He knew the doctor would be tired by the time he got to the oasis, and probably a little scared, although he'd never admit it. He would also be in pain. He could control his reactions to it, but it would still be there. He was, after all, just a man.

The doctor's breathing slowly relaxed, his chest rising and falling in a perfect monotonous rhythm as he sat quietly in the gathering darkness, listening, smelling, feeling the air for movement.

Waiting and watching, Souter could feel his legs begin to stiffen as he sat motionless. The air was cooling quickly as the night grew darker. He would need to move soon or risk the chance of his legs falling asleep. Of course, the slightest movement would alert the doctor, but that was going to happen anyway. It didn't make sense to wait until his limbs went numb. He needed to get things moving along.

"Hello doctor," Souter said calmly.

The doctor reacted quickly, spinning around to face the voice, a rock clenched in his fist.

"I knew it was you," he spat angrily. Andrew crept back slightly, kneeling behind the boulder.

"Did you, now?"

"I could smell you from a hundred yards away. Don't forget that I know who you are, you stinking bastard," the doctor answered.

"I guess you do," Souter conceded with a half-hearted chuckle. "You look good to have come so far across the desert."

"Go to hell," Andrew replied. "I'm not going back there." Every sound Souter made shot toward him as a red arrow, pinpointing his location.

"Don't be so angry at me. You knew the punishment for insubordination would be severe."

"Go to hell, you bastard. Anyone who enjoys being Savon's lapdog deserves everything he gets," Andrew said, suppressing his anger as he calculated the man's position and distance.

He knew that Souter was the recipient of the eyes that Savon had stolen from him. Many of his nights since had been spent plotting his revenge, but he never expected the chance to come so soon.

Andrew listened carefully, taking in the noise Souter made. His breaths were coming in quick, forced pants through his nose, faster than an average man at rest. The scent of his body was strong. He was nervous.

Andrew smiled but kept his attention focused on the man sitting less than twenty feet from him. He would only get one chance. Souter was a ruthless bastard. If he missed, he'd be shot and probably killed. Either way, he'd end up back at the Facility and he wasn't ready to go back just yet.

"So how long have you been Savon's pet, Souter? It's rumored that he raised you. Did he?"

"I don't see how that is any of your concern, Doctor. Just surrender peaceably and we can all be home in just a few hours."

"I'm not going anywhere. Why don't you run back to Savon's lap and let him pet your head, give you an 'attaboy' for trying."

Andrew's thoughts went momentarily to his friend, Nickodem Peterson, a world-renowned biotech engineer despite being blind for most of his life. The man taught him a great many things after Savon took his eyes, the most important of which was how to see without his eyes. Peterson's friendship dragged him kicking and screaming from the depths of depression and gave him a new mission in life: revenge. Everything since had been devoted to that end.

Many times he'd been struck by a tennis ball thrown by his friend before he learned to listen to the subtle disturbances in the air and use it to triangulate sound. The first time he caught one they celebrated with a glass of cognac. Success had never tasted so sweet, until today.

"I don't know why you have to be so difficult. All you had to do was follow orders and..." A rock the size of a baseball sailed through the air, striking the lens of his goggles before Souter could react.

A gunshot rang out as Andrew ducked behind his cover, then scurried through the undergrowth.

Souter rolled to his right and tried to stand, immediately realizing the error of his waiting. His legs were stiff and uncooperative. Cursing his own arrogance, he struggled to his feet.

Looking through the shattered lens of his goggles, he swept the area quickly to find the doctor but saw only the same empty scene he'd been looking at for hours. Now, however, there was a kaleidoscope effect showing multiple images at different angles. Switching to infrared he swept his head frantically back and forth looking for a heat signature, but the effect was the same. It would be next to impossible to catch the doctor alive now.

A knot tightened in his stomach as he thought of reporting to Savon that he'd failed. He couldn't do that. He'd have to tell him the doctor never showed and that he'd broken the goggles in a fall. Disappointing Savon wasn't an option.

Two-thirds of the way through his sweep, he heard the rustle of palm fronds to his right. Spinning on legs that still refused to work properly, he lost his balance and went to a knee, firing two shots at what might have been the heat signature of a man's torso. The fragmented glass lens made it impossible to tell exactly what he was seeing. Screaming, he fired another shot in frustration.

Andrew stood motionless, now behind Souter, holding a large rock above his head. He waited as Souter fired two shots at the scrub shirt he threw into his field of vision, and then another one in the general direction. Souter was frustrated and angry. That was good.

The sound of the glass lens of the goggles shattering told him he'd hit the target. It would be difficult to see, but he still had to be very careful. Being hit by a stroke of dumb luck could still be fatal.

The new version of the goggles was his own doing, intended to interface with the wearer's optic nerves, and he knew their weakness. Although the monolithic glass provided a better, unobstructed view, damaging it would corrupt the entire sight path instead of just one lens. He was glad they'd opted to go with simple glass for the prototype, in the later versions, the rock wouldn't have even scratched the lens.

Moving silently, holding his breath as to not alert the man of his presence, Andrew stayed just out of his field of vision as Souter turned. Going undetected wasn't hard. Souter was almost in a panic, breathing heavily and grunting in frustration. Andrew did, however, need him to speak to give him an accurate target. He had time to wait, but not a lot. The rock he now held over his head was already getting heavy.

Souter swept the area in front of him through his broken viewfinder and tried to stand again, but his right leg was mostly numb and refused to cooperate.

"Look, Doc, I never meant you any harm," he lied, watching for any movement, ready to fire. "When they decided to punish you, they were going to do it anyway. I was as much a victim as-"

Andrew brought the rock down against the man's head with all his strength. It struck with a sickening thud. The sound of the bones breaking vibrated inside his mind as warm blood splattered across his bare chest. Hefting the rock again, just in case, he listened as the body fell limply to the ground. The wetness on the rock told him he wouldn't need it again. Lowering it, he tossed it aside and knelt beside the man he'd just killed.

His hands fell on the body along the man's waist as the last involuntary spasms passed through Daniel Souter. Andrew grimaced and slowly moved over the body. Souter's clothes were better suited for desert travel; that was good. They were more or less the same size. The doctor placed two fingers alongside Souter's neck, checking for a pulse that he knew wouldn't be there.

Sitting back with a sigh of relief, Andrew stared down at the body. Not seeing it, but rather absorbing what he had just done. He'd killed a man with his own two hands. A bad man, yes, but another human being, nonetheless.

Somewhere deep inside, the man he used to be, already mortally wounded, died a quiet death. The man who had taken the Hippocratic Oath to "do no harm" was gone. He was someone else now. Who that man was, he wasn't quite sure yet.

Two thoughts entered his mind almost simultaneously, pushing out any remorse he might have dwelt on. One was that he couldn't stay here. They'd eventually come looking for Souter, and him. The second thought was one he'd had many times while contemplating his revenge.

He was taking back what was his.

Leaning over the body, he rolled the man's head to face upwards and allowed his hands to wash over the goggles as his fingertips probed angrily around the seams where they attached to the man's face.

Stitches still lined the intersection of man and machine. In time, his face would have healed and grown to the artificial skin that lined the goggles. Given enough time his invention would have blended seamlessly with the wearer. They would always look like low-profile goggles, but the integration would be sleek and smooth.

Gripping the goggles in his hands, he paused momentarily, preparing himself for the task at hand. He took in a deep breath and exhaled slowly, making sure of his grip. He took in another deep breath and snatched as hard as he could.

The goggles broke free from Souter's face with a sickening, tearing sound. In the silence of the desert, it sounded like something akin to ripping duct tape. He laid the goggles carefully aside and turned his attention back to the body. He still had work to do and wanted to finish before he lost his nerve.

Major Townley snapped to attention as General Michaels entered the room with a brisk walk. The scowl on his face said that he wasn't happy. He rounded his desk and sat in the plush leather chair before taking off his hat and running a hand over his gray, thinning hair.

"Well, lemme have it," he barked, looking over the wide desk at his subordinate.

"Yes sir," the Major began nervously. Being the bearer of bad news was never a good position to be in. "We haven't found much about the doctor. We ran the picture they sent us through the database. His name is Andrew Harkins, he's a surgeon-a pretty good one apparently-at Mercy General just outside Philadelphia. He's married to Samantha Walls Harkins, thirty-seven. One kid, a son, Lane Thomas Harkins, six years old. As far as anyone knows they just disappeared four years ago. No sign of them since, well, until our friends found him in the desert. The coordinates are in the report, but it was just north of the Yemini border in Saudi. The group that found him was on a night training mission."

The General leafed through the report, shaking his head, and grunting at the news.

"He's just some run-of-the-mill surgeon who disappears for nearly four damned years and ends up in the middle of the freaking Saudi desert?"

"We're in touch with the Saudi ambassador to see if he had a work visa. Nothing yet on that, sir."

"How in the hell is that possible? Freaking bureaucrats. Shit. Any involvement with any of the known terrorist cells?"

"No sir, intelligence has been all over his life, social media, friends, extended family. There's nothing to indicate any involvement whatsoever. As I said, he and his family more or less disappeared and have been radio silent since then. No contact with family, friends, nobody."

"No indication that he was a player, for anybody? Not even us?" the general asked.

"Nothing at all, sir. CIA, FBI, Secret Service, Intelligence all claim not to know him."

"They would. What about MI-6? Russians? The Israelis?"

"Nothing, sir."

"The fucking circus? Boy Scouts? Anything?"

"Sorry, sir. Nothing."

"Then how in the hell does an American doctor end up in the middle of the desert, blind as a bat, and carrying..." the General looked over the file laid out before him. "A pair of fucking eyeballs! What kind of bat crap crazy shit is that?"

"I'm not sure, sir. We're still gathering information. Right now we don't know if he was dropped there, or if he was wandering the desert. They did say there were no signs of a wheeled vehicle anywhere near him when they found him. There were footprints, but they weren't able to follow them far. The wind, sir. As far as they could discern, he walked to where they found him."

"What is near there?"

The major shook his head. "Nothing within walking distance."

The general shook his head. "Nearly forty years in now, Major. Forty years, and this is the weirdest shit I've ever seen. What the hell do you think happened to the poor bastard?"

"I don't know, sir. Something awful. It's too bad we won't get a chance to ask him."

"That's what has Washington in a tizzy. How the hell does a blind man escape anybody? And in the condition that he was in, dehydrated, half-starved?"

"That part is still a little disjointed, sir. The person who examined him thought he was dead. The report said he wasn't breathing, and they couldn't register a pulse. They sat him aside and made calls to find out what to do with the dead body of an American civilian. Naturally, they were a little nervous about the whole situation. And things are a little unsettled over there, to say the least. Sir."

"Nothing on the family?" The general asked, closing the file.

"Nothing out of the ordinary. They're looking at all known relatives, but so far nothing."

The general pursed his lips and shook his head again, lost in thought. "Well," he began with a sigh. "At least it was some friendlies who found him. Hopefully, he wasn't into too much deep shit in Yemen. That's all we need right now."

"Well, sir, if he was it looks like they handled it. If he pissed some people off, I'd say they got their revenge."

"You never know, Major. There's a lot of crazy folks running around that part of the world."

"I'd hate to think you could do worse to a man than cut out his eyes, stick them in his pocket and leave him in the middle of the desert."

"Is that what you think happened?" the General asked. "He was just wandering around the open desert and dropped dead?"

"Pretty much all that makes sense, given the circumstances. But apparently, he wasn't as dead as they thought."

"Apparently. I'd like to find out just what happened and who the hell he is."

"Me too," the Major agreed. "I'm sure we aren't alone in that either. I've been getting calls all day about this guy."

"Of course, this is all quiet. The last thing we need is an American running around stirring the pot over there. Or getting himself taken hostage and having his damned head cut off on the evening news."

"Yes. Will that be all, sir?"

"Yes, Major, that's all." As the Major left the room, the General leaned forward, propping his elbows on his desk, and rubbed his temples. Looking down at the file, his eyes went to the smiling face of Andrew Harkins. In his late thirties, with a head full of brown hair and two rows of perfect teeth, he hardly looked the part of an international terrorist organization. Maybe an agent, but even that was probably a stretch.

"Who the hell are you, Andrew Harkins?" he asked. "And what in the hell happened to you?"

Made in the USA
Middletown, DE
19 July 2023

35454541R00146